GUARDING HIS RUNAWAY PRINCESS

THE STENISH ROYALS BOOK 3

JAYNE KINGSLEY

BLUEBERRY LANE
PUBLISHING

To my gorgeous bestie, Naomi. Thank you for always believing in me.

THE STENISH ROYALS SERIES

Sweet contemporary royal romance that will leave you breathless and dreaming of another world.

Stenaco—a small European country nestled amongst mountains and rich with life—is home to the Stenish Royals: Crown Prince Henrik, Prince Felix, and Princess Isabella. After the devastating loss of their mother, these three need to find themselves and learn to trust love again, often in the most unlikely of ways.

ABOUT THE AUTHOR

Jayne Kingsley writes contemporary romance filled with fashionable and fun heroines and the hunky heroes that capture their hearts. She currently resides on the picturesque south coast of NSW with her two young daughters and her own real-life gorgeous hero.

She loves connecting with her readers. Head to www.jaynekingsley.com to sign up to her newsletter, or join her official facebook page.

1

Princess Isabella wiped the trickle of sweat from her brow. It wasn't that hot out. Summer in Stenaco hadn't reached its full potential, but her body was slowly heating from the inside—a tell-tale sign she was being forced to do something uncomfortable. But she would do it. For her father, and her siblings, she would try.

Taking the last step, she entered through the side door and halted. Across the stage was the man in question, King Bastian. He was conversing with both her brothers, Henrik and Felix, and their significant others, Eva and Sophia. The men all wore their dress regalia, medals glinting as they moved. Both Eva and Sophia looked resplendent in complementary pastel dresses—demure yet ever so stylish. Izzie glanced down at her own outfit. Her dress was maroon, the royal family's signature colour. It should have made her feel part of what she was about to walk into, but it just left her even more isolated.

She shooed away the thought, her gaze lifting again to the group only steps away. It was like a scene from a Hallmark movie. Happy couples holding hands whilst they laughed with the man of the hour. Her father, who had no trouble giving each person who spoke his full attention—he looked each of them in the eye as he listened and answered —not an ounce of uncertainty or blame in his expression.

Something within her rolled over. Another wave of heat danced down her spine. Her father never looked at her like that. He never spoke directly to her.

Have they even noticed I'm not there yet?

Her brain took a snapshot of the blissful scene before her and played out the movie of what would happen if she walked forward and joined them. How her presence seemed to suck the air from the room when she and her father were both there. How, no matter what she did, he still couldn't bear to even look her way.

Today's event wasn't unusual—the opening of the Summer Festival. But having the entire royal family in attendance was. Izzie tried to take that step, to propel her body forward towards the gathering. Her legs were lead. The heat that had been threatening drew closer, and she was in trouble.

She stumbled back.

Ian placed a steadying hand at her shoulder. "Princess? Is everything all right?"

His words were comforting, but his presence wasn't. She didn't want anyone to see her like this. Ian had been her bodyguard since she was in nappies, and had looked after her mother. At least he had before she'd taken her life. They'd lived through that ordeal together, and no matter what, he'd always be there for her. The silent father figure who comforted her more than her actual father.

But not even he knew of her minor problem. A problem that was becoming far more frequent and far more pressing.

"I have to go."

Her words were breathless, air refusing to fill her lungs that burned for that sweet freshness. The command to her limbs hit its mark, finally allowing her to brush past the older yet solid form behind her, propelling her through the door and out the back of the stage. More bodyguards stood at the entrance, giving her a brief nod but not questioning her frazzled and almost drunken movements. Why couldn't she move anything properly?

It had been weeks since this had last happened. Why now? Why today?

Her thoughts scattered, desperation to be alone taking over all else.

"Princess Isabella? Are you ill?"

Ian's voice again. His hand cradled her elbow to guide her away from the side entrance. She could hear voices calling, laughing, could smell the festive food in the air. All normal things. Maybe if she could focus on just one normal thing, she could hold this at bay.

The eerie noise beckoned, her head collapsing into one giant ache. She scrunched her eyes tight, trying to block the noise with her hands over her ears like she'd done when she was four and hadn't wanted to listen to a berating.

Then her world went black.

She came to, her eyes taking in the pale beige carpet above her. Why was there carpet above her? *You're in a car, silly.* The motion and whizzing sounds were unmistakable. Sitting up, she held her head. "Ouch."

The car slowed a modicum.

"Princess Isabella, lie back down. You blacked out. I'm taking you to the hospital."

"No! Just take me home." Silence met her request. "I mean it, Ian. Take me back to the palace. That's not a request. It's an order."

Their eyes met in the rear-view mirror, his edged with crinkles of concern. She thought she caught the start of an eye-roll, but he glanced away.

He didn't answer, but inclined his head, indicating to turn the car around towards the palace. Not answering wasn't good—that meant he was angry with her. And if he was angry with her, she could only imagine what her father would be.

She didn't care. She forced herself not to. Instead she took Ian's advice and laid back down. Perhaps that would help flatten his feathers a little.

That one scene back at the festival had broken her. How did seeing her family all so happy—without her—cause such a reaction? Was that even normal?

No. It's not normal. That's not what brought on your anxiety attack though, is it?

She huffed, shaking off her thoughts.

The black sedan slowed. The slight scrape and whir of the electronic gates told her they were close to home. The car sped up the long driveway, the occasional blip of branches breaking her view of the pristine blue skies. She sucked in air, pleased when it didn't catch in her throat. Her lungs ached from the deprivation earlier. Her mouth felt funny too.

Maybe Ian was correct, and she needed to go to hospital, but she couldn't. Something told her this wasn't a medical issue so much as a mental issue.

Her brain was broken.

Her emotions were screwed.

I am a walking liability to the family.

Ethan Raines glared at his commanding officer. Gardening leave? What on earth was this? He didn't work in some damn office.

"Could you repeat that, sir?"

"You're relieved of duty. Not forever, but currently, you're a liability. You won't take the hints we've given you. You won't let this case rest. It's time we took the next level of action."

Ethan ground his teeth in a way that had him mentally apologising to his dentist. He gave a curt nod. "Understood, sir." He peeled his frame up to a standing position and walked out of the room.

He congratulated himself on not smashing his fist into the wall on his way out.

Months of work brought undone by a situation out of his control.

One more deep breath, and he pushed the anger aside. It would do him no good. He'd learned that the hard way. But unlike most, he never repeated a mistake twice.

He was a trained, elite protection agent, and he'd do as he was told.

Perhaps it was time to take a holiday. The ski-trip deals to New Zealand his mum had emailed him this morning sprang to mind. Sydney in winter was okay, but nothing to write home about. Queenstown beckoned—pristine fluffy snow and ice-cold beer were enough to seal the deal. If he couldn't work here, then he'd darn well go elsewhere to burn off his energy in another way. *Screw it.* He'd go home, book the next flight, pack a bag and his ski gear. This time tomorrow, with any luck, he'd be carving up some of that powder the Kiwis were always bragging about.

Izzie stormed into her father's office. There he sat. The King of Stenaco.

"Not now, Isabella. I need to go over this speech for tomorrow evening." Her father didn't so much as glance her way.

Not anything out of the ordinary there.

Well, not this time. This time, she'd make him hear her out. "Yes, now, Father. When am I going to get an answer from you?"

He placed his pen back against the desk with a subtle thud. He exhaled as if he shouldered the weight of the world, not a simple question regarding Izzie's future. "When I believe you're taking the situation seriously."

He held up a copy of yesterday's paper, a tabloid that had a tendency to print trash, one that regrettably featured her own delirious face on the front cover. Her dress was hitched to the side showcasing her underwear, and her mascara had smudged in a way that was less smoky siren and more drunk panda.

"That photograph was taken months ago."

"When you were in Greece, having skipped out on tasks that I'd delegated to you, right after your brother's wedding. You want me to take you seriously, yet you pull stunts like this?" He stabbed a finger right on the image of her face, finally looking up from his desk. Tired blue irises bored into hers, laden with sadness. When he flicked his gaze back to the paper, he physically flinched.

That one movement hurt worse than a bullet. Worse than the words he'd just thrown at her. It was an emotional punch she hadn't been ready for. How often had her father really looked upon her for more than a moment since her mother passed?

Her brain refused to compute that information.

She took a seat in the chair that faced his desk. "I know my behaviour has been bad, but I want that to change. I'm ready to get back on track. You've let enough stuff slide with Felix and Henrik. Why are you always so much harder on me?"

He didn't answer. The injustice was like acid on her tongue. As usual, his treatment of her stood out as another dismissal of her place in his life.

After what seemed an age, he sat back a little in his leather chair. "And today? Was that your idea of being ready to get back on track? Ian told me you fainted. Refused to go to the hospital. What was it this time, Isabella? Too hungover? Drugs? Drunk at eleven a.m. when the rest of your family turned up to officially open the Summer Festival? You say you want to change, but I don't believe you."

Izzie couldn't look at his face anymore. Even without eye contact, his disapproval radiated towards her, condemning her without a chance of rebuttal.

"It wasn't any of those. I skipped breakfast and felt a bit off, that was all. It won't happen again. Can't you see I'm trying?"

Her eyes fell to the pen that sat on top of his hand-written speech. He picked it up, twisting it around before dropping it back to the table. It was practically identical to those that Henrik and Felix both had. Heavy gold with their names inscribed in flowing script along the body. Gifts from their mother only months before she ended her life.

Izzie had also received one. But hers was hot pink, the end filled with crystals that sparkled whenever she used it.

Completely fun and frivolous, exactly what Izzie preferred in her stationary.

She swallowed back pain. Margot had bought one the same for herself, but in royal blue. They'd been two peas in a pod, and that loss of support hurt like a nail through her heart. Her mother would understand her actions, her behaviour.

Fed up with waiting, she pushed the chair out—the loud screech somehow pleasant compared to the loaded silence.

After marching out of the room, she pulled the door shut behind her. The wood went *thunk*, creating a slight echo through the corridor.

Well, booey to him.

Yes, she'd acted like an immature idiot since her mother passed. She wasn't the only one. What twenty-three-year-old princess would cope after her mother swallowed an entire bottle of sleeping tablets and lay within the depths of her own especially designed rose maze, waiting to be discovered? It was like the stuff of fables.

Without warning, her knees gave out and she fell in a crouch, her eyes slamming shut. Her body actively repelled the memories that would appear out of nowhere, assaulting her with what would never be.

Was it any wonder she'd spent the past five years running from anything and everything?

Just like this morning, the panic mounted. Her breathing was shallow, but no matter what she did, she couldn't suck in deeper breaths. Her eyes blinked open, but her vision blurred, nothing making sense except an urge to flee.

What did they say about trauma victims? Fight or flight?

It didn't seem worth fighting it anymore. It was time to go away.

For good this time.

The plane taxied along the runway, the flight having been short and smooth, just as Ethan liked. Flying wasn't his favourite thing. Every time he stepped foot on a plane, he felt helpless. No gun or combat skills would help him if the plane just fell out of the sky. A ridiculous concept perhaps, but one he couldn't shake.

A dainty foot in heels, tapping to an unknown beat, caught his eye. It wasn't the first time he'd noticed her, and anticipation was coiling in his gut at the prospect of seeing what the rest of that foot led to. A flash of blonde ponytail had occasionally peeked out the side of the seat that was three rows in front of him. The diagonal view had given little away, but it had entertained him for the past thirty minutes since his movie had ended. Not that Uma Thurman wasn't captivating, but something about the woman ahead intrigued him more. So much more.

For one thing, who wore three-inch strappy stiletto heels into Queenstown? It was snow season, and they'd be landing late evening, which meant temperatures in the negatives. She appeared to be wearing skin-tight jeans and some loopy jumper, but nothing that spoke of sub-zero wear.

The plane jolted to a stop. Passengers jumped to stand even though the seat belt signs glared their backlit message to remain seated. He mentally shrugged, in no hurry to follow the crowd. Miss Stiletto hadn't stood either.

The man beside him shifted closer, warm expelled breath hitting his cheek. Without moving, his eyes tracked to the inconsiderate idiot beside him. It did the trick. The poor dude's face paled a shade or two and he shifted back into his own personal space.

Giving it another few minutes, allowing the young, harassed mother with two whining children to stand and move off, he followed suit.

His gaze traced ahead along the aisle. *Damn.* His interaction with close-breath man meant he'd missed his opportunity to see Miss Stiletto stand. Never mind. He'd catch up with her at baggage claim. Or if she'd already gone, then it didn't matter. He was here on holiday. For once, he had no one to protect, no one to investigate. Nothing but a few weeks of solid relaxation before him.

At least, that was what he kept telling himself, ignoring the niggling in his gut that said otherwise.

2

———

*I*zzie tried to relax against the pleather seats of the taxi. At least, she was fairly sure the seats were pleather and not leather. They didn't smell like the real deal, though it was a little hard to tell over the cigarette-infused car smell.

It had been a while since she'd gone travelling incognito. She was rusty. To blend in, she'd have to do a much better job. Particularly the shoes. When she'd asked for the next available flight to the other side of the world, Queenstown, New Zealand, had sounded cutesy and idyllic. The reality was butt-freezing temperatures and icicles on the trees. The air had a real freshness to it, though, that wouldn't be ignored, and already she breathed easier.

Hooking a strand of hair behind her ear, she congratulated herself on her quick getaway. Her newly purchased and boring khaki bag had been waiting on the twisty thing at baggage claim. The blue tag bought at Geravia airport was gimmicky. The souvenir shop assistant had barely glanced at her as she'd handed over the cash. She guessed the black bob wig had worked there.

Close to twenty-four hours of travel later, she'd been ready to climb the walls. How on earth did anyone travel like that? It was preposterous. It was all in the name of a break though.

With an alternative name and a new phone number, it would take Ian a while to track her down, and that was if her father bothered to send him. Blocking that thought, she fussed in her bag—vintage Chanel—probably something she should have left behind. But, well, some things couldn't be parted with. Finding her phone, she waited for it to load and locate its fresh place in the world. A message flashed on the screen: *new SIM detected. It should read new life detected.*

It beeped a few times. Izzie gripped the phone tighter, her heart rate erratic at the thought she'd already been found. *Nope. Just more SIM notifications.*

She went to toss it back into her bag just as a tinny bleat assaulted her eardrums, its musical atrocity indicating an incoming call. Desperate to make it stop, Izzie swiped before gingerly placing the phone to her ear. "Hello?"

"Is this Izzie?" It was a man's voice, but not one she recognised.

"This is she. You are?"

"Holding your bag."

It took her a moment to register his words. The smooth-like-chocolate tenor of his voice had distracted her, making her imagine ... things. He sounded delicious. How she'd decided that from six words was beyond her, but hey, maybe the fresh air was already doing the trick.

"Holding ..." She looked at the bag on the seat beside her. It was khaki, and the right size. The blue rose mocked her as she flicked it over. *Ethan Raines.* "Oh. I picked up the wrong bag."

"It would appear so. If you give me your address, I'll come to you to swap back."

She swallowed. No go. She didn't want to give her address out—even if his voice sounded all types of delicious personified. She'd just have to ask the driver to double back. "No, it's fine. Are you still at the airport?"

"Yes."

"Wait there. I'll come to you."

She clicked the red end button, not waiting for him to agree.

Ethan frowned at the disconnected call then shrugged off the odd feeling of anticipation. He'd known the bag wasn't his when he'd flicked the tag over to check. Long-time habit —check all the facts.

Having nothing better to do, since his hire car keys were already in his jeans pocket, he headed to the bar to order a beer and wait. He selected a chair that gave him an excellent view of the entrance.

Not more than twenty minutes later, he spotted her. Miss Stiletto strutting back into the terminal, his khaki bag in tow. She walked with an effortless glide that spoke of money and prestige. He considered her clothes casual, but the way she wore them was far from that.

And still with the heels. He shook his head, the corner of his mouth quirking a little.

She paused when she was about five metres away from him, her head swivelling, her gaze taking in the area but not finding what she looked for. He leaned back in his chair and used his foot to shift her bag forward a little.

Sure enough, on the next lap she caught sight of her bag.

Her gaze shifted to him and her delicate brows arched a little. *Bingo.*

It didn't take long for those shapely legs to deliver her to his side.

The corners of his mouth pulled into a smile. He leant forward and held out a hand. "Ethan Raines."

She hesitated, her eyes flicking between his face and the hand held out to her. *Odd reaction number two.*

"Izzie," she said after another beat. Her hand slid into his much larger one, and her grip was firm.

He nodded his chin at the chair opposite his. "I can give you a lift back to your hotel if you want to take a seat? I won't take long to finish this beer."

"You'd offer a perfect stranger a lift?" Her voice held a funny edge, but she sat down.

"I think I could take you if you tried anything."

Her eyes narrowed, like she'd taken his words as a challenge, not the joke he'd been attempting.

"How did you know you had the wrong bag so quickly?" She crossed her legs in a smooth move, bringing his attention once more to the heels. Her posture was very uptight though. A woman of mystery and suspicious of him. He'd bet a hundred bucks on that fact.

Something about her reaction made him want to rile her up, loosen the cool demeanour she'd had on like a cloak from the moment she'd sat down. It was annoying him.

"Your lingerie." The words slipped out before he censored them.

"What? You opened my bag?"

He shifted his gaze from her shoes to her face, into her startled ocean-blue eyes. Her mouth gaped a little.

He laughed, unable to stop himself. "Nah. I'm kidding. I checked the bag tag."

"You're not funny."

"I guess not."

She tapped the table with a purple fingernail. It matched the soft colour of her jumper and her heels.

He took a sip of ice-cold beer, the tangy, bitter flavour sliding down his throat. Her next words collided with his swallow, and he was thankful he didn't choke.

"I don't want a lift. I'd just like my bag back please."

Though surprised by her words, he didn't let it show. "Why did you sit down?" He leaned over and collected her bag, swapping them in front of her eyes. "I wasn't holding you here."

"You're Australian?"

"That's why you stayed? You couldn't place my accent?"

"No. You remind me of someone."

"Who?"

"I'd like a drink."

He let his eyes rove over her face. Her expression hadn't changed, but he felt the subtle command in a way that spoke of her being used to getting what she wanted regularly. She was captivating, beautiful and elegant. But that wasn't why he wanted to get to know this Izzie better. It was what she wasn't saying that was playing havoc with his insides. "What's your poison?"

Her eyes narrowed. "Champagne. That's not a common expression."

He stood. "It isn't?"

Walking away from the table, he went to the bar to order her drink. From the corner of his eye, he could see her flick her bag tag over and then lean over and do the same with his. He understood her interest. They were identical. Though his was faded and old. Hers appeared brand new.

Tapping the EFTPOS machine, he nodded his thanks to

the woman behind the bar and returned to the table, placing Izzie's glass before her.

"I'm afraid it's not the proper stuff. It's called sparkling here. You're from Europe?"

Her accent sounded slightly British, but then not. The way she lilted her T's and F's made him pause on his calling her from being from London. She wasn't backpacking. Just what brought the mysterious Izzie to Queenstown? And how'd she end up with a bag tag identical to that of his late father's? A tag he'd told Ethan was from his time in Stenaco.

***

Izzie took in the rugged features of the man sitting across from her—deep chestnut hair, tall yet lithe frame, and green eyes that shone with a rakish gleam that bumped him from being an eight to a solid nine.

"Yes," she replied in answer to his earlier question. Europe was a common assumption. She had no plans to share more than that. "What brings you here?"

"The snow. You?"

"Change of scenery. Where is your bag tag from?"

"My father."

Izzie frowned. In Stenaco, the blue rose symbol was common, but she hadn't ever noticed it other places. Was his father from her homeland?

"You're frowning again," he murmured.

She deliberately smoothed any expression from her face, collecting the glass and taking a deep gulp of the over-aerated liquid. The faint acidity of a too young vintage burned her throat, and she wrinkled her nose to dissipate the feeling. "Is there a law against it?"

"I guess not. You're a bit of a puzzle, Izzie."

"Do you like puzzles?"

The corner of his mouth quirked, her eyes drawn to the move. She wasn't sure if it was the accent or just his general way, but he looked incredibly comfortable with himself. What she wouldn't give to feel that sense of confidence again. That sense of freedom. He didn't appear to have a care in the world. She took another sip of her drink, waiting for an answer.

"Depends on the puzzle. Long way to come for a change of scenery."

"I like the cold."

"That would explain your choice of footwear." His tone was dry.

Is he being funny? She hadn't missed the glances he'd thrown at her shoes. He was hard to read, not at all like anyone she'd ever hung out with. He wore no watch, and his jeans were worn at the knees in a way that spoke of actual wear, not carefully styled attribution. His T-shirt was plain black, and the hooded sweatshirt worn over it had no label, no subtle branding. And were they hiking boots?

He wasn't anything like the guys from her world. A fact that gave him more appeal than it probably should since her reason for being here was to sort her head out. Yet ... maybe a carefree dalliance would help cure her of this clutter in her mind that refused to leave her alone.

"You don't like my shoes?" She arched her foot then twirled it around, adopting an artfully confused yet innocent expression.

"It's below zero outside."

"How astute and nice of you to worry. But I'm a big girl. I can take care of myself."

She'd expected him to smile or say something cute. Maybe to ask something else about her. His lips barely even moved. The only hint that he'd recognised her brief flirtatious moment was a subtle shrug of his broad shoulder. He drained the rest of his beer before placing the empty glass back on the table with a soft *thunk*.

"Since we've established we can both take care of ourselves, do you want that lift?"

"Actually, I really want fries."

"Fries?"

"Yeah, you know—potato that's been fried in oil?"

He gave her a funny smile before shaking his head and heading towards the bar. She picked up her glass and drained the contents. Why had she prolonged this? She knew nothing about this guy, other than he was hot and had strangely boring taste in luggage. Something about him though ... or was it just that for the first time in a while she felt a sense of rejuvenation? There was no looking over her shoulder, no watching what she said or how she sat in case there were cameras waiting to capture an off day. Not a single soul knew where she was. She'd paid darn good money for the fake passport that had given her this choice.

The passport was something she'd had for a while, arranged after her first ... attack? Episode? Hell. Izzie didn't even know what to call them. All she knew was that she was desperate to make them stop. She was desperate to find a way back to her old life—the safe and happy life she'd had prior to her mother's suicide.

Shivers spilled down her spine along with an emptiness that left her gasping. Just thinking that word made her want to retch.

A glass was plonked in front of her, its ruby red contents heralding a soft fizzle that reached her ears.

"Sparkling shiraz. An Aussie one, but I think you might find it preferable."

Izzie tilted her head, pleased that he'd taken the time to notice she hadn't really enjoyed her last drink but also perplexed at how easily he'd read her. "Was I that obvious in my distaste of the other?"

"No."

"You're not a man of many words, are you?"

"Not when one will do. Chips won't be long."

"Thank you. What do I owe you?"

He shook his head. "You returned my bag—we'll call it even. Do you ski?"

"Sometimes." She didn't elaborate, her thoughts about skiing uncomfortable.

A lock of her hair slid out of her ponytail. She reached up to flick it away but caught the table with a *bang* and sent her glass flying. "Crap!"

Ethan lunged forward, catching it before it fell, though not before half the contents splayed across his wrist.

She jolted. "Wow, that was quick ..." Her gaze shifted from where she'd been staring at his arm to his face that looked a little rattled. A pulse throbbed in the base of his throat.

"Are you okay?"

He righted the glass onto the table. "Sure. Just a spilt drink."

Why didn't that ring true? It hadn't been the glass flying that had him moving. It had been the loud sound. "Those are some crazy-fast reflexes." She let out a short, barking laugh. "Don't tell me you're a cop or something?"

"Or something," he answered, but his eyes slid from hers.

A waitress came over with their food and a few extra napkins that she handed to Ethan with an inviting grin. It seemed Izzie wasn't the only one to notice his scruffy, hot factor. Her smile widened at the thought.

"Guess I better not ask you anything else about snow sports—we might lose our food next."

"Funny—" she began when a buzzing and lilting jingle interrupted her.

He shifted, pulling his phone from his pocket. "Sorry, I better take this. It's my mum."

Izzie couldn't stop the pang those three words caused. Belatedly, she pulled a smile onto her face as he answered the phone. Had he noticed her hesitation? She reached for a chip. Her fingers burned a little at the hot oil that still seared the shard of potato, but it didn't deter her. She welcomed the pain to take her mind off feeling anything else.

Unable to block out his voice, she gave in to curiosity and shamelessly listened.

"Yep. No, Ma, you don't need to go over. My neighbour will take care of it."

He scratched at his jaw before he shifted in his chair. His fingers stretched and curled against the tabletop. He had enormous hands. In fact, Izzie was looking forward to seeing him unfold his frame to its fullest.

"I don't have a fixed date." *Pause.* "Yeah, the flight was fine. Hit some turbulence just after take-off." His nose scrunched, and she caught the tail end of a tiny eye-roll. "Yes." *Pause.* "Nope."

He looked up suddenly, catching her in the act. Instead of looking away in embarrassment, she held his gaze. Something about listening in to his conversation that to anyone else would seem boring, was anything but to her. How nice it must be to have someone in the world who cared that much to call to check you arrived at your destination okay. He grinned with a conspiring gleam in his eyes. Something inside Izzie went clunk. *Wow.* Just where had he been hiding that sparkle?

"Yep. Love you too." He hung up before re-pocketing the phone. He shook his head with a softer version of the smile he'd just thrown her. Happiness was invading the guarded persona he'd been holding onto since she'd met him.

"Sorry about that. My mum." He shrugged like that explained the phone call, but she detected a tiny tinge of pink at the top of his cheeks. "She worries."

Izzie's normal reaction would have been to say something flippant or a touch of teasing. But that short display of phone conversation told her that whoever this guy was, he loved his mother dearly. "You're lucky."

He leaned in, grabbing a handful of chips before shoving them all into his mouth at once. He raised a brow at her in question.

"My mum died five years ago." The words were out before she could call them back, but something about saying them was cathartic. Perhaps it was the telling a complete stranger angle. Her eyes darted behind him, suddenly wary of her oversharing such a personal comment before they were drawn back to his soulful green eyes. Was it his eyes that had made her want to spill part of her broken life? Their deep green seemed to look past what she showed everyone else.

Izzie, you're a mess.

He gulped his mouthful. "That's rough. I know I'd be lost without my mum. I lost my dad when I was eight. It's not something you ever fully recover from, losing a parent before their time."

His words sent shivers spilling throughout her insides. For the first time in a long time, someone's response to her mother's death didn't make her want to gag. He understood.

There were no false platitudes or insincere remorse. Or the worst reaction, where they looked at her with such pity. Like they could see the event had completely broken her. That was always unbearable.

"Tell me about him." Izzie sipped her wine, enjoying the creamy fizz as it glided down her throat. He was right. It was a million times superior to her prior drink and far more to her taste. She could get used to this Aussie stuff.

"He was a bodyguard. Actually, that's how he met my mum. He was on an assignment in London. She was there on a working holiday. They met, travelled to Australia so he could ask my grandpa's permission to marry mum, and within a month they were married. When I was three, we shifted again for his work to a small country just near Denmark. Stenaco, it's called. According to my mum, what they had was genuine love—one in a million." He laughed at himself, the move endearing even though every one of her muscles had clenched and her breathing had seized.

Did he know who she was?

Surely not. It had to be just a ridiculous coincidence.. It would explain the bag tag.

She grabbed her glass and took a larger swallow than planned, forcing the liquid down her throat without choking on it.

Opening her mouth to claim no knowledge of her home country, she changed her mind at the last minute. Something about this Ethan Raines made her not want to tell him even the smallest of white lies. He seemed too honest. Too ... pure. "True love. At first sight?"

"According to her."

"You sound a little sceptical on that part."

Again with the nonchalant shoulder shrug. That habit could become annoying on most, but Izzie suspected with him it could be pure torture. Every slight movement made her want to witness the play of muscles underneath his clothing. *Get a grip, Izzie.* This holiday wasn't about finding some hottie to hook up with. It was meant to be about finding time to sort out her muddled brain.

"I believe in taking things step by step."

She'd almost forgotten what she'd asked him, but the way he narrowed his eyes at her told her he hadn't. Though he also didn't appear to have any issue with the implied double meaning to his words.

It was time to leave. A glass and a half of alcohol after all the travelling she'd done had taken its toll.

After grabbing one last chip, she popped it into her mouth. "Thank you, but I have to go."

She stood and he rose with her, the move smooth yet seemingly ingrained. Her gaze travelled high. Even in her heels, he towered over her annoyingly petite frame. What she wouldn't give for a little more height. Another family trait her brothers were both gifted with that she'd missed out on.

"I'm happy to give you a lift."

"No. I'm good." She dithered with her handle, uncertain on how to play this now that she'd stood. She didn't really want to go, but she needed sleep and time to straighten out her head. A six-foot-plus tall, dark and handsome package didn't feature in those plans. Finally, the handle clicked and she could pull it up.

She met his gaze, waiting for him to say ... something. But he remained silent. His face gave nothing away, though his eyes had tiny creases in their corners, narrowed ever so slightly.

Her smile cracked a little under the pressure of that gaze. Spinning on her stiletto heel, she walked away. Three brief steps and some pronounced hip-swaying later, and she gave up the act. Stopping, she pursed her lips then turned enough to cock her head over her shoulder. "I really like ice cream."

His lips quirked, amusement lighting his features.

"Guess I might see you around, Raines."

Without waiting for a response, she resumed her strut towards the exit. After a beat, she thought she heard the muttered words, "You can bet on it."

3

———

The icy air blasted Ethan's face like tiny pinpricks. His morning run was a lifestyle choice, and to keep his fitness up for work. Without it he was irritable, as it freed his mind, clearing up all the twisted knots from the day before. This morning, however, his mind wasn't filled with recent cases—in particular his last client whose death still gripped him—it was filled with a five-foot six package of pure delight and intrigue.

Izzie.

No last name.

That point alone had sparked his interest. It was unusual to put only your first name on your luggage tag if you planned to also use your mobile number. Mentally he shrugged that away—could just have been that she'd run out of room or was going for a super-famous-pop-star angle. Though that didn't ring true. She had style and exuded a level of class reserved for the mega-rich, but she wasn't trying to be noticed.

In fact, if he had to put money down, he'd say she was doing the exact opposite.

Any time he'd asked a personal question, she'd steered the conversation back to him. With the one exception of her letting it drop that her mum had died five years previously.

A tough break for anyone, but in her he'd sensed that wound ran deep.

There was one other tiny titbit he'd been fed—her penchant for ice cream. An open-ended invitation to track her down if ever he'd heard one. There was only one place in Queenstown to go for ice cream—so hopefully that was where she'd head.

Reaching the top of the incline, he breathed hard, his lungs burning with his efforts. His original plans to hit the slopes first thing had been pushed back. He just couldn't get her out of his mind. She was a mystery to be solved, and he welcomed the distraction from the other more pressing mystery in his life. That of his stupid enforced work break.

His gaze slid across the valley before him. Lake Wakatipu's water glinted with the first rays of the rising sun. Puffs of mist evaporated before his eyes from his hot expelled breaths. It wouldn't pay to pause here too long, given the temperature, but the view was magical. He jogged on the spot, little side steps and hops that kept his heart rate ticking over at speed and the chill from seeping into his bones. Time to make the descent towards to the apartment he'd rented for the week.

By the time he arrived back, his cheeks could have chilled a beer to perfection. He flicked on the kettle, needing caffeine to warm his insides and filter into his brain. A shower beckoned, but he pushed himself to wait until he'd completed a series of sit-ups and push-ups. A holiday wasn't an opportunity to slack off.

With muscles that ached in the best way, he took his steaming coffee to the glass sliding doors that led to the deck. His mum would probably call again today, just to check in. She said it was for him, but he knew it was for her. His mouth tilted into a smile, as cerulean blue eyes shaded by thick lashes sprang into his mind. Izzie's interest in his call to his mother had clung. Her face a picture of intrigued curiosity that she'd just given into. He liked that she'd done that. She hadn't pretended to not listen when she blatantly was. She'd owned her choice in the situation.

It had been a while since Ethan had felt any spark with a woman. Hell, his last relationship had been years ago. The timing never seemed right. He travelled a lot and well—the job always came first. His dad might not have been part of his life for as long as he'd wanted, but he'd left a lasting mark. Ethan knew what it took to be the best at his game, and he planned to ensure he'd do just that. Like his father had.

Throwing back the last dregs of coffee, he returned to the kitchenette to rinse out his cup. His normal routine back home would have him heading off to work. The odd feeling he had about his out of the blue dismissal grated, digging a hole in his mind. Yes, he may have overstepped the mark on his last case. A guy had died. On his watch. A fact he hadn't been able to let go. Still couldn't.

He itched to call Cameron. While his friend may not like it, he'd be able to give him an update on how the official investigation was going. Ethan knew in his gut that something wasn't adding up about that case. His dismissal yesterday only added to that. Back home, it would only be about four in the morning. Hell, he was on holidays—he should sleep in. But he hadn't been able to.

Grabbing his ski jacket, he headed for the door. Time to indulge in something greasy for breakfast. Then he could turn his attention to a task that was causing far more excitement than it should—that of hunting down ice cream and a certain blue-eyed blonde.

Izzie gulped down a breath of icy fresh air. Queenstown had been delivering on the relaxation front since she'd finally arrived at her destination. Her gaze roved around the courtyard of her rental house, the ground partially covered with patchy white mounds of snow.

Her old phone had rung half a dozen times since she'd switched it on briefly to collect a few bits and pieces to transfer onto her temporary phone. And to send a single message to Sophia, letting her know she was safe and to tell the others not to worry. After the third call from her brother Henrik and the fifth from Felix, she'd switched her old phone off again. *Back in the land of anonymity.*

She wasn't trying to frighten them. Or pull some stunt as one message she'd glimpsed had implied they'd initially thought. She just wanted time to sort her head out. As things stood, she was a walking liability, and she didn't know how to explain that to any of them. Thoughts of sharing her issues left her feeling short of breath and her gut sinking to her toes like a lead balloon.

No.

She would justify her actions later. Right now, she was exactly where she needed to be. Besides, they had seemed to cope perfectly fine without her in the past.

That sounds bitter. I don't want to be bitter.

Her eyes scrunched tight, blocking out the unwanted thoughts. She was well aware her behaviour was coming across as a little petulant from where her siblings stood. But she couldn't find the words. How did she go about rationalising her emotional turmoil to anyone when she didn't even know how to sort it out in her own head?

Mentally pulling up her big-girl pants, she physically shrugged. It was time to find ice cream. With any luck, her mysterious Ethan from the airport might even be there to join her. Not that he was hers.

The metal latch on the gate was so cold it burned her fingers as she dropped it back into place. The walk into town wasn't far, and thankfully it was downhill on the way there. The ground was wet from melting snow and she took care not to skid on any of the icier-looking parts. Not one pair of shoes she'd packed had a flat sole, which meant shopping was on her horizon—a pleasure she was looking forward to.

It had been a while since she'd gone shopping incognito. The last time had been ... with her mum. She swallowed back acid. With her mind racing and her breathing shallow, she stopped and dipped her head towards the path, hands locked onto her knees to steady her position. Nausea swam, and the blackness threatened. Tiny spots danced in her periphery.

One tiny thought. One tiny memory. And she was all but confined to the spot.

"I don't think you're going to find any ice cream in the footpath cracks."

It took her a moment to place the voice. Somehow she used its familiarity to pull herself back from the edge. She straightened, tucking a loose strand of hair behind her ear before focusing on the man before her, hitting around his stomach. Her gaze travelled up for a while before it fastened onto dancing green eyes that sparkled back at her.

"Are you stalking me?" she quipped with a smile, buying herself time. At least the dizziness was fading, the spots dissipating.

He lifted the skis he carried, then shrugged. "I think I'd choose slightly more inconspicuous gear, but whatever floats your boat. You heading into town."

It was less a question and more a statement. His eyes narrowed a little on her for a moment before they cleared again. It was that move that shifted the last of the darkness away from her. Seeing his face had jolted away her panic. Because he was attractive and she didn't want to appear like a fool in front of him? No. That didn't seem right. She'd had attacks when surrounded by others before. Where she'd had to claim drunken stupor to ward off unwanted questions and concern.

No wonder her father thought she was a walking joke and wouldn't look her in the eye.

Ethan bent at the knees, claiming her gaze when his eye level reached hers. How did one look ask everything and say nothing? And make her feel safe. She shivered. "I need to go buy appropriate clothes so I can eat ice cream."

Her lips spread wide in answer to his knowing grin.

"If you give me a minute to drop this gear off, I'll join you." He didn't wait for an answer, just jogged past her, up the hill and over the road to the apartments about half a block from her rental house. Interesting that they were in such proximity. Serendipitous?

She liked his attitude. Or was it his confidence and strength? He wasn't threatening. She could easily start walking off and she got the feeling he'd get the message and just leave her alone. But he appeared to have judged her enough to know what she wanted. And what he wanted.

Before long, his tall frame appeared from the wooden deck that featured at the front of his block. His long stride ate up the distance in moments. He wordlessly handed her a pair of charcoal gloves.

Reaching out, she clutched the soft knitted yarn, rubbing her thumb across the surface. "Thank you," she murmured before slipping them on. Immediate warmth cocooned her fingers. "These are gorgeous."

"Possum gloves. Your fingers were turning blue."

"Aren't you observant?" She hadn't meant to sound so tart.

"With you, yes. I won't lie, Izzie. I find you highly intriguing."

Her heart stuttered, partly as she enjoyed being intriguing—to him—but also because that meant she was standing out. She didn't want to stand out. "I'm not that interesting."

"Perhaps I should be the judge of that. So tell me, why are you really in Queenstown?"

"You don't believe I'm just here on a holiday?" She tilted her head in his direction, a brow raised, but she didn't quite look him directly in the eyes. He seemed to see far more than he should.

"You strike me as someone who is fairly level-headed, yet you arrived in the evening wearing sky-high strappy heels that left your toes out in the cold. And today you've ventured out in just a jumper, high-heeled boots—no gloves or scarf. I'm thinking you either packed in a hurry or weren't fully thinking through the move. Or had no idea where you were going. Either way—none of those options speak planned holiday to me."

"Perhaps it was one of those holidays where you pack a bag and turn up at the airport to just jump on the next plane, regardless of the destination."

"I imagine you would have said so if that were the case." His eyes slid to hers. The corner of his mouth lifted in amusement. "No matter. You'll either tell me the truth in time or you won't. I'd like to add that I'm an excellent listener."

Izzie soaked in his words, weighing up the options in her mind. It was tempting—unburdening to a perfect stranger. Except it wasn't a feeling she'd ever experienced before, which told her it had less to do with him being a perfect stranger and him being just ... well ... him.

The first shops drifted into view as they neared the end of the street. A few ski-hire places ran alongside a lane. She'd scoured a map earlier this morning and that lane would bring her out onto one of the main strips of town. If they kept walking towards the marina, they'd find an ice-cream shop.

"Should we head straight for ice cream?" she said, ignoring the sense of his heavy gaze that she could still feel penetrating the side of her face. He might be a wonderful listener, but no way was she ready to be an honest talker. Not yet, anyway.

"Let's get you a proper ski jacket or coat first. Then we can eat while walking around the lake. The other side leads into the botanical gardens, which is a pretty chilled walk."

"Guessing this isn't your first visit here?"

"Nah. I come most years or whenever I can. If I can't get here to ski, I ski at home."

"Australia has snow?"

He gave her an amused look. "Yes. We have snow. Where in Europe specifically did you say you were from?"

They'd reached the strip of shops, and having walked past the first two which held only ski hire, Izzie targeted the third which looked to be more general clothing for sale. She pushed open the door, beating Ethan to the task. "I didn't say," she quipped over her shoulder.

"There's that aura of mystery again. For someone who claims to be boring, you're falling short of the memo."

She hummed in an uncommitted fashion, moving about the shop. Her eyes narrowed in on a jet-black puffer coat. It looked warm and long and the fur collar was cute. That would do. After grabbing a size 8, she shrugged it on over her jumper and zipped up the front. Her body welcomed the warmth immediately.

"Nice," Ethan said.

She glanced up, catching the slight frown spreading across his dark features.

He lifted the corner of his mouth. "Is this the part where you tell me you couldn't possibly buy the first thing you tried on? That you must check at least half the stock available in case something else is more perfect?"

Her nose twitched. That was exactly what she'd normally do, but in this case she made herself not care. This was a purchase based on weather. It was not like she had to worry about how she'd look in any media photos. She resisted the smile that wanted to break free at that thought.

The only person who semi-knew her stood right before her, the slight gleam of appreciation in his green eyes telling her he'd meant every smidgen of his compliment, and that was good enough for her.

Ignoring the slight look of surprise on Ethan's face, she marched over to the cashier and paid for the jacket using a debit card in her fake name. The wind chill outside had picked up a little, biting at her skin before she had removed the tags and put her new coat back on.

"That was ... decisive."

She ignored the unspoken question. "I wanted ice cream. Besides, you don't strike me as the shopping type."

"No. I'm not. Guess I better buy the ice cream then. To say thanks."

Her eyes skittered sideways, a small smile forming. "Is that your subtle way of asking me on a date?"

He turned left, his fingers brushing hers and loosely clasping her hand to tug her along after him. "Nope."

He'd pulled them into what looked like a walkway between the shops. A shortcut that opened back out onto another street. The lighting was a little dim, but she glimpsed water in the distance. His fingers slid against her hand, his thumb doing a gentle dance with her thumb. The touch was slight, but it sent little shivers up and down her arms. She sidestepped, bringing their bodies into alignment. Her eyes only reached his chest, even in heels. She followed the stitching line of his jacket, counting each stitch in time with every stroke of their fingers. It was ... hypnotic.

She sucked in air through her nose, drinking in the dark fragrance that was slowly infiltrating her senses.

"Izzie?"

His voice tugged at her mind, dragging her away from her assessment of his scent. Her eyes floated upwards, hovering on his lips, which twitched at the corner. She was stuck on that view, on the soft yet inviting pink of those plump lips. She wanted to kiss him. God, why? This was not an ideal time to be feeling an attraction to some stranger.

He ducked, his knees bumping against her thighs, bringing their eyes to a level footing. He grinned a full knowing grin that spoke of mutual attraction and desire. "Just so we're clear. You'll know when I'm asking you on a date."

She blinked. Either she was rusty or he had some serious self-control. Because from where she'd been standing, that had been the perfect opportunity for him to kiss her.

"Come on. Ice cream awaits." He started walking away but didn't let go of her hand.

Now who is being mysterious and difficult to read?

4

———————

*L*ake Wakatipu held a glassy sheen. The wind brushed in soft sweeps across the surface, but wasn't enough to disturb the serene facade for long before it resettled into perfection. Ethan had always loved Queenstown. Something about the atmosphere here was relaxing. Back home, his life was far more ordered.

After fishing his phone out of his pocket, he glanced at it, confirming that there'd been no recent calls or messages. His boss had probably been right—maybe he needed to let go of the case. Just chalk it up to one screw up amongst an otherwise perfect record. He reached across to rub at the newly healed bullet wound within his shoulder.

Izzie's hand squeezed his, her voice light. "Is something wrong with your shoulder?"

He dropped his hand away. "Old injury. It tingles in the cold sometimes."

"Tingles? What's the injury from?"

What did he normally tell people? This wasn't the first bullet he'd had imbedded in his skin, though he sure hoped it would be the last. His first had been a rookie error from a friend during his time in the army. The wound was a reminder he'd messed up. He'd missed something.

He missed nothing.

"A work thing," he said at last.

Her eyes shifted sideways. A slight frown dipped into place as she looked at his shoulder, then his face. "If you don't want to tell me or can't, you can just say so. You said you were a cop. I get there are rules."

"Actually, I'm not in the force. I work for an elite protection agency."

Her hand jolted.

"Protection agency." She stopped walking.

He shifted so he stood before her, their hands still linked, but he could feel her drawing away from him. *Odd.*

"You're a bodyguard?"

"Yes. Why does that scare you?"

Her eyes darted away, and she swallowed. Her shoulders shifted slightly to the left, like she was trying to hide her thoughts. He waited, mentally begging her to be honest with him. He hadn't planned to tell her. Not that his job was a state secret, but whatever this thing was between them, he'd thought it would be light. A bit of fun. Yet in the brief time he'd been in her presence, he was slowly being drawn further under her spell. He wanted to get to know her. He wanted her to trust him. *Why does that matter to me so much?*

After what seemed an age, Izzie shifted her stance around so they stood toe to toe. She looked deep into his eyes. It was a move that left him feeling a little dizzy. He'd been stared down by some of the most powerful people in the world, yet none of them had left him a touch short of breath.

"Are you working right now?"

He didn't understand why she'd ask that, but he instinctively knew his answer was very important to her. "No. I'm on leave. My last job ... something went wrong, and I ended up shot." He tilted his head to the shoulder he'd been rubbing before. "Apparently I don't do rest and recuperation the right way, so my boss ordered me to take a break."

She snorted. "Now that I can definitely believe. You don't strike me as someone who does anything half-hearted."

"That's quite an assessment for someone you barely know."

"It is, isn't it? I guess you just have a protective aura about you. I felt that the first time I met you. Even with your size and dressed as a gangster, I didn't feel threatened. In fact, oddly, I felt safe."

He stowed that information to ponder later. Did that mean she normally felt threatened? Just what was Izzie running from? Or whom?

A bump from behind had him shuffling his feet forward a smidge. "Let's go. We're kind of in the thoroughfare here."

The ice-cream shop sat just off the main square facing the water. He pushed the door inwards, ushering Izzie in before him, out of the cold. Heat engulfed him the moment the door swung shut behind him. It was the one thing about snowy locations that bugged him. Outside you'd freeze to death. Inside you'd die of heat exhaustion. Surely there was a happy medium there that was being missed.

"What's your flavour preference?" he asked. Izzie was pouring over the selection like a kid in a candy store.

One assistant came over to serve them. "You can try any of the flavours first if you like?"

He looked at Izzie, but she seemed well in the zone.

"I'll have a single-scoop chocolate cone. Izzie?"

"Um. Gosh, it's impossible to choose. What are you having?"

Yep, definitely in the zone. "Chocolate."

"Okay. Well, I can try yours, so I'll go with a double-scoop salted caramel and coffee, please."

The assistant seemed a little dazed by Izzie's smile. He couldn't blame the poor kid. She really did have a cracking smile when it's full force of sunshine was aimed your way. In fact, he hoped to enjoy it being aimed his way a little more often.

Ethan leaned against the nearest chair whilst they waited for their orders to be served. "So you're just assuming I'll share?" he asked with a cheeky grin.

She widened her eyes, their blue irises shining with humour. "Only if you're willing."

He got the feeling Izzie knew exactly how to play to her strengths and get what she wanted.

Collecting their cones by mutual agreement, they wandered back outside. Her hand brushed against his thigh and he switched his cone to his other hand so he could capture her fingers as they walked. "So do you have a last name at least? Even if you're not willing to share your exact home location."

She laughed. "Isn't a bit of mystery fun sometimes?"

"I suppose so. I guess it depends on the reason for the mystery."

"My brother just married the love of his life. They met as complete strangers and their lives were a mystery to each other for years before they were drawn back to one another. I think when it comes to the heart, it's okay to be mysterious." She paused, her brows furrowing. "Not that I'm implying we're heading in that direction."

Ethan enjoyed the slow spread of pink across her cheeks. "If you've got a thing for me, you could just say."

She spun in front of him then, pinning him with those baby blues. "That's a two-way street. I'm old-fashioned. I believe it should always be the man to admit defeat first."

His mouth twitched, unable to help himself as he leaned in close so only centimetres separated her mouth from his. He ached to close that gap. God, she was something else. Had he ever met anyone who had his insides tied up in such delightful fun?

She didn't budge, taking a delicate nibble of her ice cream which left a smidge of white on the corner of her mouth.

"You've got a bit …" He flicked his gaze to her lips then back to her eyes. Eyes that were swapping out the cheeky gleam for an edgier raw hunger. They searched his, their focus darting between his eyes, as if wanting an answer to … something. Shifting his weight, he detangled his fingers from hers and used his thumb to wipe away the skerrick of ice cream, before putting it straight into his mouth and sucking off the flavour with a pop. "Salted caramel. I'd better try that one next time."

Should he kiss her? His body was screaming yes, but something was holding him back. He wanted to know what she was hiding. Her evasion with anything personal was becoming an obstacle. Was she in trouble?

Or was she just trouble?

Izzie refused to back away. Ethan was deciding whether to kiss her. She could see the indecision in his eyes, could feel the tension in his torso even though they no longer touched.

"I'm from Stenaco," she murmured after what felt like an age of staring at each other.

He didn't move, but she sensed the change in him. "Stenaco. My dad was born there."

Her brows shot up, surprise radiating through her. "That's quite a coincidence."

"That it is." He inched forward. Izzie's pulse beat faster, delicious anticipation coursing through her veins with every millimetre that was closed between their lips.

An ice-cold drip landed on her thumb, but she ignored it. The taste of her ice cream might be sweet, but she had an inkling it would be nothing compared to the taste of this man before her.

His phone buzzed, stilling his movement. "Hold that thought. I better take this."

Her breath hitched, telling her she'd been depriving her body of actual air intake. *Nice work, Izzie.* She was off-kilter. Ethan Raines was ... different. She wandered a scant distance away, giving him some space to take his call. His quiet tone reached her, but his words were too muffled to determine.

She attended to her ice cream, collecting the drips from her fingers with her tongue. The salty and sweet taste had lost its appeal. The coffee underneath was too bitter. She bit into the cone, at last finding comfort in something crunchy that she could sink her teeth into. Edginess crept in. The realisation that she was walking a fine line. Hadn't she run away to be alone? To sort out her mind and find a solution to her problems? She hadn't come here to fall for some stranger.

Not that she was falling.

She swallowed, trying to bring moisture to the arid interior of her mouth. What were the chances she'd travel to the other side of the world and meet a bodyguard whose father came from her own country? It rattled her. The coincidence sat heavy. Except his answer about not currently working rang true. She believed him. Her imagination was running away with itself, finding problems that weren't there. One thing she knew for certain is that she hadn't felt this connected to a person in a while, this relaxed and being able to just be herself. Maybe it was time she let down her guard and opened up a little more? He didn't strike her as someone who was out to use her, or expose her for his own gain. He was just a guy on a holiday from his job.

Ethan frowned at the voice that came down the line from the private number. It was a voice he hadn't heard in a while.

"Ian. It's been a long time. To what do I owe this pleasure?"

"Ethan. I'm sorry to bother you on your vacation, but I have a favour to ask."

Unease crept into Ethan's chest. Ian Hart had been one of his father's best friends, but it had been years since he'd heard from the older man. Something about his tone told Ethan he wasn't going to like the favour.

"News must travel fast," he said with a touch of suspicion. "My holiday was a spur-of-the-moment decision."

"I'm not tracking you if that's what you're implying. I called your mother to see if you were on any important jobs. It was she who mentioned you were in Queenstown."

"And this favour involves what, exactly?"

"I need you to monitor someone."

"No can do. I'm on a holiday. According to my superior, I need the time out."

"I wouldn't ask if it wasn't important. She's an important figure, and something tells me she's in a lot of pain. I need someone I can trust looking after her."

Instead of easing, his chest tightened like a noose was slowly being drawn about his neck. Last time he'd spoken to Ian, he'd been part of a royal family's protective unit. The Stenish Royal family. Ethan would let a little coincidence slide, but this was starting to rove into territory far past chance.

He looked over at Izzie, taking in every inch of her perfectly poised form. *Surely not.* "What's her name?"

"Isabella. But she's better known as—"

"Izzie," Ethan dead-panned, cutting off the other man.

"Yes. Princess Isabella of Stenaco."

Silence and thousands of miles stretched across the phone, a dread stealing over Ethan. "Blonde, petite, elegant and has a penchant for inappropriate footwear?"

"Sounds like you've already found her."

"I'm looking at her, yes. Just what the devil are you playing at here, Ian? This feels like a set-up."

"Never mind that now. Just monitor her. Do not let her out of your sight, and whatever you do, don't tell her about this. Please?"

"Why?"

"Because she's running from something, and no one knows what. I'm worried if she finds out we've tracked her down, she'll just run farther. I need your word on this, Ethan."

"You have it." The words were automatic.

"I reckon she'll talk to you."

"Why is that?" Ethan asked.

"Because you both have misguided views about your fathers."

Ethan barely had time to register the words before the line dropped dead. What the hell did Ian mean by that? Ethan didn't have a mistaken view on his father. The man was a hero, and the best darn bodyguard around. Or he had been. He'd died protecting what he believed in—his job. Sure, it had been tough growing up without him, but he was the man he was today because of his father. There was nothing misguided about that.

His arm dropped away from his ear and fell to his side as he gripped the phone tightly.

Ethan's stomach plummeted. He couldn't act on his growing attraction to Izzie now. He'd just taken on the role of her protector—falling for her was out of the question.

He gritted his teeth, pushing back thoughts that he should confront her and own up to the deception he'd just agreed to. She was a princess. What the devil did she think she was doing, gallivanting about by herself halfway around the world? Stenaco might be a small country, but even he knew the royal family were richer than Croesus. She was a walking international incident waiting to occur.

Loosening his fingers a little, he raised his phone and tapped out a message to the last known number he had for Ian. If he was going to take on this role, he needed all the information available to ensure he didn't miss a thing.

Walking over to Izzie, he pasted a smile on his face. It wasn't like he'd kissed her—even if every fibre in his body had wanted to. He hadn't crossed the line.

"You look like you've eaten dirt," she quipped.

Ethan smoothed the frown from his face. He needed to get a grip on his emotions. There'd be plenty of time for him to explore this revelation later. Right now, he wanted to continue the subtle seep of information she'd been issuing him.

"Just a work thing," he said in answer to her quirked brow. It was the truth. She didn't need to know that the work thing was, in fact, her.

5

—————

By mutual agreement they started walking around the lake, towards where Ethan had pointed out the botanical gardens. It had been a while since Izzie had just wandered aimlessly, with nowhere to be and no schedule to follow. It was peaceful.

Ethan had been a little off since he'd taken the work call. Something about the way he looked at her ... there was a slight change there that she couldn't quite define. Or was she imagining things? She'd felt off-kilter ever since she'd locked gazes with the emerald depths of his eyes.

She'd been sure he was going to kiss her on their way to get ice cream, and again just now. Was she losing her touch? The media portrayed her as the ultimate party girl—loose, wild and free. Except she wasn't free. And she wasn't loose or wild. She was lost. All those stunts had been to get a reaction from her father. For him to look her in the eyes again and really see her. Not just see the blame he'd misplaced at her feet.

Her heels clipped against the cobbled stone path that wove uphill.

"You going to be okay walking around in those heels for a while?"

The corner of her mouth lifted in amusement. "Honey, I could run all day in these heels."

"Really? You could run *all* day?"

She chuckled. He had her there. "Okay, well in theory, if I *could* run all day, I would be fine to do so wearing these. But yeah, I guess I shouldn't claim any running prowess."

Not on the sports field, anyway.

Her phone vibrated and she frowned as she pulled it out of her pocket, recognising Felix's number immediately. *How the hell?*

She hit decline, shoving the phone back into her jeans.

"You don't need to get that?"

"No." She shook her head, emphasising her point, but smiled at the frown creasing Ethan's eyes. "Just my brother. I'll call him back."

"So you have a brother. Does he know where you are?"

"Why would you ask that?"

"You said this was a spur-of-the-moment holiday. Time to find yourself. Remember?"

Had she really told him all of that? "He's not my keeper. I can take care of myself."

"Of course you can. Mind you, you might want to dial down the defensiveness. I was only asking."

Oh, that grin. *It's not fair!* How long had she lived her life with friends bemoaning her brother's cheeky playboy grin that promised all sorts of trouble—their words obviously, not hers—but it wasn't until this moment that they made sense to Izzie. Because right there, on Ethan's face, was every reason to dive headfirst into another way to take her mind off her own problems.

"Sorry. I didn't mean to sound defensive. He's older.

Actually, I have two. They are both older. And yes, I may be a little defensive with them."

"Why?" His face showed nothing but open curiosity.

How often did she get the chance to talk about her family with any grain of truth? Without a chance of repercussion or flak from anything she said, without looking over her shoulder for a camera.

She'd always had to watch her words.

Her brother Felix's girlfriend was probably the closest thing she had to a best friend. But not even with Lady Sophia could Izzie be totally honest. What if she misconstrued the words? Took them out of context? Izzie had learned that lesson early when the Stenish Royal Herald had printed quotes of her saying things about her father out of context. It had been just after the funeral … She shook her head as if to ward off the memories, and the other feeling that had crept in.

Her skin chilled.

She wished she'd not eaten the whole two scoops of ice cream. The sickly sweet tang of salt and caramel churned in her belly like a whirlpool. *Not now. Please.*

Her eyes slammed shut and her footsteps faltered.

"Izzie?" His voice held concern as it floated into her mind from far away. "Izzie!" This time it was louder and accompanied by his hand gripping hers. The pressure locking against her fingers snapped her eyes open again, her senses returning to normal. She blinked into his emerald gaze, dazed by the heat and concern she saw there.

"Sorry," she whispered.

Without another word, he pulled her into his arms. Warmth seeped into every pore, grounding her into the actual world, away from her memories that were threatening to consume her with darkness. She dragged in a deep breath before blowing it out noisily through her mouth. Yoga breaths. She'd found over the years they helped to calm her accelerated heartbeats.

"Talk to me," he said at her ear.

She shook her head. But for the first time, she wanted to. She wanted to unburden this secret she'd held onto for years. She wanted to unburden herself of the guilt and the blame she felt whenever she thought of her mum, or looked at her dad.

Burying her nose against his chest, she drank in his smell. Cinnamon and spice, mixed with something else that she was coming to recognise as purely him. Was that normal? She'd only met this guy yesterday, yet already she'd be able to pick him out of a line-up blindfolded.

God. She needed help. She was being sappy. *Pull yourself together, Izzie. No one likes a broken and sad girl.*

"You don't need to apologise. Ever." He shifted away, his palms sliding up her arms to grip her shoulders gently, his eyes locking onto and never leaving hers. It was like he could see straight into her soul. His strength transferred to hers and somehow a tiny broken piece of her was knitted back together.

She offered a lopsided smile—the best she could manage. "I'm not normally this ..." There was no word that fit. Stupid? Broken? Weak?

"Do you get along with your brothers? Is that what brought this on?"

No judgement. No questions. No crowding her or demanding she go to hospital to be checked out, asking if she was drunk or what drugs she'd taken. Just acceptance and concern. She tucked those thoughts away to analyse later. "No. It's not related to them. Well, not really. I love them to pieces, and they are brilliant brothers, if a little overbearing. But that goes with the territory, right?"

"I don't know. I'm an only child. But I imagine if I had a younger sister, I'd be ready to protect her at a moment's notice."

"You'd be every younger sister's dream—strong, silent but considerate. Of course, she would hate you because all her friends would have fallen for you. So probably better for your sake you don't have one."

His cheeks went a tell-tale shade darker, and he squirmed. "I'm not really that sort of guy. To be honest, my last few relationships have died in the water. Apparently I'm married to my job."

"Yeah. I can't say I've had much luck either."

"I find that hard to believe."

"I—" She paused, realising she'd just been about to tell him that being a princess had some serious drawbacks. She shrugged, buying time. "I guess my job gets in the way too." That sounded believable.

"What do you do?"

She wanted to slam her palm against her forehead. Of course he'd ask that. She'd lead him right there. "I studied international relations. I'm hoping to go into diplomacy."

"Hoping to? That doesn't really answer my question."

"I'm in the family business. I guess you could say my father doesn't believe I have what it takes to be a foreign diplomat. He wants me to stay as I am."

"And you don't want that?"

No. She didn't want to stay in this stagnant life she led. She wanted to go back in time. Needed to. To before she'd lost her mind. "It's not the worst job in the world, but it's not what I'd hoped for my life."

"Can't you just tell your dad that?"

"Ha! If you'd met my dad, you'd know it's not that simple." She looked over at him, thinking she'd find him smiling, but was surprised by the odd considering expression that graced his face. Little creases bent between his brows and his lips were flat.

"Tell me about him."

They started walking again, but she noted he walked a little closer this time, as if offering support in the form of his body for her to lean on if needed.

"He's ..." Just how did she explain he was the king of a country—a country Ethan appeared familiar with, without giving her identity away? Something told her it wouldn't matter to Ethan, but she wasn't ready to take that chance. She liked the way he looked at her like she was just a regular person. There was no deference or watching his words, no trying to find an angle to get something from her. "He has a powerful job that takes up most of his life."

"Does he enjoy it?"

Good question. "I assume so. I've actually never asked. It's a family business. I'm not sure he had any choice." Her brows knitted together. She hadn't ever stopped to think about whether her father enjoyed the position he held.

Growing up, the prospect of living life as a glamorous rich princess had distracted her. In her late teens, early twenties, the shine had dulled a little on that idea. When the realisation that people had stopped treating her as Izzie kicked in, instead only as Princess Izzie, she'd shifted her focus to studies. Sure, she'd still partied and enjoyed her life, but she'd become wary of who she trusted with what information.

She'd trusted her mother.

They had been inseparable, and she'd shared her hopes

and dreams with her. Hopes and dreams that seemed to have died with the queen.

"You've gone quiet again. Do you know you spend a lot of time in that head of yours? Thinking, thinking." He smiled, his words not harsh or judgemental, just stating an observation.

Since meeting him, she had been spending a lot more time thinking about her life. And her choices. "Thinking is exercise for the brain."

He laughed at that, revealing a dimple in his right cheek. She reached up and swiped at the dent, the stubble scratchy under her thumb.

"How do you feel about another sort of exercise?" The gleam in his eyes had her figuring his actual and implied meanings were different.

"Depends what it is. I might be persuaded."

"I'll give you three guesses. It involves ice."

She noted the sizeable building that they were coming upon on their walk. "Ice skating?"

"Bingo. You're good at this guessing business. So how about it?"

She ignored the dull thud of disappointment in her stomach. Ice skating was fun, but it wasn't exactly what she'd hoped he'd been referring to. "Can you skate?"

"Don't know. I've never tried it before."

It was her turn to laugh—a deep chuckle that bordered on devious. "This should be fun."

Who in their right mind did this? Pain shot down his left thigh as his skates yet again flew out from beneath him.

He'd learned fast that falling to his side was preferable to his tail bone.

"Ouch. You ready for a break yet?"

His eyes tracked the graceful glide of Izzie's form as she circled around him and then bent to offer a hand. He waved her away, not wanting to pull her down with him when he next fell. Statistically, the chances of that were around one hundred per cent.

"I'll admit, I may be ready to claim defeat. How do ice-hockey players make this look like a breeze?"

"I'd suggest the hours of training and lifelong commitment would be an excellent start, but I don't want to ruin your dreams."

"It's okay. I'll be crossing this off the list. How long have you been skating?"

The ice rink was bare except for them. Izzie floated around the rink, her movements confident and beautiful. The angle of her foot switched, and she spun on the spot at rapid speed before pushing off again to come back to where he still sat on the ice. He eyed the distance to the exit off the ice, weighing his options. Crawling would be hideously embarrassing, but he wasn't sure he could handle any more bruises.

"Since I was three."

"And you're how old exactly? Mid-twenties?"

"Twenty-eight."

"So you've had twenty-five years to look that good on the ice. My chances are definitely shot." He dug the end of his blade into the ice and pushed himself towards the exit. He couldn't allow himself to crawl.

"C'mon. Let me help you off the ice. Then I figure I better buy you a drink."

"Does it come with an ice pack?"

Setting his feet onto the solid ground was one of the best feelings ever. *Give me skis and powder over that any day.*

"Is now a terrible time to mention that this was your idea?"

"No. But next time I have some random idea to try something new, please remind me of this."

She smiled at him, her eyes fresh with excitement, her features relaxed. It was a good look on her, like the activity had eased some of whatever had been twisting her in knots.

They sat on the benches, carefully swapping out the rental skates for their own shoes. Her phone buzzed. This time he noted the international number that flashed on her screen. She just stared at it for a bit before switching the whole thing off.

This time he didn't pry.

Better he wait until he had more details from Ian before he pushed her further. The last time he'd headed conversation towards her family, she'd looked like she was hyperventilating, or had experienced the first twinges of a panic attack.

Why?

The question gripped him. He'd never been very good at walking away from an unsolved mystery, and Izzie was a whole barrel of them. And he'd promised to protect her, which meant he couldn't allow them to delve any farther down this other rabbit hole that they'd been circling. He needed to take a step back and rearrange his thoughts from interested man to trained bodyguard.

"Is there any chance we could rain check on that drink? I think I need to go soak my sorry bones for a bit."

Her eyes darted his way as if she'd been lost in her own thoughts and was struggling to place their current conversation. "Drink. Yeah, sure." She paused, clearly considering her words. "In fact, tomorrow might work better for me. There are a few things I need to do."

He frowned, noting the change immediately. She was drawing back from him. He wanted to reach out and take her hand, to explain he really did just need a hot shower to ensure his muscles didn't seize up after the brutal attack they'd just taken, but he thought better of it. This morning, when he'd run into her, he was a free man on holidays with all the time in the world to relax with a beautiful but unknown woman.

He'd agreed to protect her. From what he did not understand, but even if the details weren't concrete, even if he refused any payment for doing this favour for an old friend of his fathers. He'd taken her on as a job, and nothing ever impeded his work.

Not even if her tight smile and sad eyes begged him to choose otherwise.

6

Izzie had begged off leaving the ice rink after Ethan's announcement that he had to bail.

Really, she shouldn't be surprised. She'd all but panicked in his face after knowing the guy for barely a few hours. He probably thought she was some deranged, pathetic looser.

He'd asked for her number, but would he call her? Gosh, how long was it since she'd been ice skating? The rush, the cold, the ability to fly. She'd kept her moves basic, not wanting to appear as if she was showing off. Besides, after this long, her muscles were too weak to perform any jumps or difficult spins, but it hadn't stopped the feeling of exhilaration that had raced through her the moment her boot had hit the ice.

Ice skating had been another of those things she'd done with her mum. They'd gone every other week, her schedule permitting. She could remember her father laughing about building an indoor rink just for them. He hadn't understood that part of the fun was leaving the palace. That for a brief period, they could just be normal people, skating in a public arena.

It wasn't until after her mother had taken her life that Izzie understood just how much that escape had meant to her mum.

And why she'd not returned to skating in the years since.

Memories of angry words assaulted her. Her words—thrown in a fit of spite over something so trivial. Her decision to walk out and get drunk with friends rammed home just how young and immature she'd been. Why hadn't she paid more attention to what her mum was saying? Had she even changed since then?

It really was no wonder that her father didn't feel her fit for the role of foreign diplomat. Just what proof had she given him she could do the job? Hell, she couldn't attend a family gathering without a panic attack.

Her heart clenched.

After ramming her feet back into her skates, she tied the laces with practised precision—her fingers flying at double speed, all whilst she fought back the demons that wanted to take hold of her mind.

Gliding back onto the ice, a tear slid unbidden down her cheek. The music switched from some pop star rapping about drumsticks to an eerie love ballad. It suited her mood perfectly. Love lost and then found. But different. She danced to the music, feeling it through every move she made as her body executed moves without thought.

This she could do. This she remembered. A time before it had all gone wrong, and she'd screwed up everything.

Her mother's death couldn't be laid at her feet. She hadn't given her mother the bottle of pills or forced them down her throat. But she'd walked away after an argument, after words had been exchanged that could never be absolved or taken back. An argument about a boy—her mother's words, which had become truth. She'd left with the last memory of Queen Margot's normally crystal blue eyes, which had been murky and beaten. The next time she'd seen them, they'd been lifeless.

She missed a beat. Her blade nicked the ice and she went down hard. Her body jolted, the reverberation of pain felt in every joint, every muscle, every sinew. The ice burned through her jeans.

A door closing sounded in the distance. Unable to move, she stared at the ice, the various grooves and blade strikes within the crystal surface. Her shoulders slumped forward, her legs spread wide. To anyone coming through the door, she was probably doing a mighty fine impression of Eeyore the donkey, sad and slow.

Shoes appeared in her periphery, shuffling with great care across the ice.

She could smell him before the warmth of his hands pulled her into a standing position.

"You came back?"

"It would appear so."

The distance was still there. It was in his eyes. The sparkle might still be on his face, but it wasn't fully reaching his eyes.

"I changed my mind about the drink."

"That's really why you came back?"

He searched her eyes. His hand rubbed at his jaw, as if deciding what to say next. "I'm worried about you."

Her muscles tightened, and she shrugged away from the hand still holding her arm. She skated over to the side, ignoring the ache in her left ankle. She'd injured it when she was younger—it was one reason she'd never gone the professional route with figure skating. It would never be strong enough, and whilst the injury hadn't bothered her in years, her fall had aggravated it.

For the second time in the past hour, they sat side by side on the bench. But without the exhilaration and chance of something that had hung in the air earlier. She didn't need a guidebook to show her the signs. Ethan might have originally found her attractive, but after her moment of panic and showing her weakness, he was withdrawing. Now he just 'worried' about her. God. She did *not* need anyone else worrying about her.

"You're annoyed." His voice was grim.

Izzie scratched at the back of her neck before turning her attention to the second skate, pulling at the laces with undue force. They were wet and sticking, only proving to further frustrate her. "I don't need someone to babysit me, Ethan. You didn't have to come back on some misguided idea that I can't take care of myself and need protecting."

He shifted at her words. "That's not—it's not why I came back. Being concerned isn't the same as being protective. In fact, in my job the two are usually on opposite sides." The last he muttered.

Was he frustrated with himself for caring? Was that what this was about?

"Let me ask you this—what happened on the walk here? Your face went paler than anything I've seen in a living person, and you couldn't hear me to begin with, like you'd disappeared into your mind."

She shrugged, waving her hand in the air. "It wasn't anything. I just felt a little lightheaded for a moment. Too much ice cream."

"That's bull. This isn't something you just brush off. Don't you think it's fair for me to worry about you, given the circumstances?"

She swung towards him, his face bare inches from hers. She could pick out little bits of gold amongst the green in his irises. "What circumstances, Ethan? We're not anything to each other."

"We aren't?" He challenged, before his gaze dipped to her lips.

She shuddered, but it had nothing to do with the chilly air and everything to do with the heat that had exploded in his eyes. A heat her body matched with every breath she took. Desire slicked through her torso. She leaned in a little more, his exhalation hitting the side of her mouth. It was infinitesimal, but he shifted a little away, then back in, as if fighting some internal battle.

Well, maybe she'd take the option from him.

Closing the tiny gap, she pressed her lips to his, finding his smooth and cool. It was only a light peck, before she pulled away a little, her lips lingering against his. She touched her tongue gently to his soft bottom lip. He nipped at hers, playful. Her eyes fluttered closed as he pressed her closer to him, his mouth dancing with hers in a soft and unassuming way.

Her heartbeat was a treble, skittering and unable to find a sense of normalcy. Her stomach swooped in delight as he changed angles, deepening the kiss a little, swiping his tongue inside to tangle with hers.

How long had it been since she'd enjoyed the simple pleasure of kissing a guy? A man. One who made her feel ... everything.

That thought caused her to scrunch her eyes tight and pull back a little.

He was being real. But she wasn't. He had no idea who she really was.

He had no idea she was a princess and was running away from a perfectly glorified life.

How could she start something with him when that lay between them like a beacon, signalling an oncoming freight train, awaiting a crash?

Ethan called himself every different version of fool under the sun.

Why had he gone back?

Why hadn't he kept walking away, like his brain had continually shouted at him with every step he took back towards the ice rink? He'd let her get under his skin. Those eyes that had looked at him with amusement, but then just as quickly turned into a pit of sadness that he couldn't shake from his mind.

Kissing her was ten different types of wrong. It was crossing a line that he'd never crossed. Hell, he'd never had an issue with following the rules and doing things by the book. Why the heck couldn't he do so now? He should call Ian and tell him this was wrong. That whatever the problem was, he needed to assign one of his own detail to this task. Ethan wasn't fit for the role. His error blared like a siren in his head.

Izzie had seemed as confused as he by their kiss. He wasn't the only one who'd back-peddled at a great rate of knots. He wanted to talk to her, to see how she was feeling, but similarly he was too scared to broach the subject.

They'd hobbled to the front, to the waiting taxi that drove them across town and deposited them at their respective places. Knowing she was mere metres away wasn't helping with this situation. Nor had the steaming hot shower he'd taken to sooth his busted body. The heat had only inflamed his other issue, until he'd turned the jets to straight cold, which had practically frozen his appendages off.

He rubbed a hand across his chin, sighing at the simultaneous aches in his thigh and shoulder. He grabbed some arnica cream he'd picked up from the pharmacy yesterday before rubbing it into the scar that graced his left side, just above his bicep. The wound was healed but still hurt like a mother of all things. He squirmed. Was he losing his touch? First the bullet on a routine protection service, a job that should have gone off like clockwork but hadn't. Now today?

The ringing of his phone was a welcome interruption. "Raines."

"Ethan, it's Ian. Do you have time to talk?"

"Yes. But only to say I can't take the job. Izzie ... I just think you need to find someone from your own detail."

There was a loaded pause. Ethan could almost hear the clogs of Ian's brain turning over that information. "Has something happened?"

"No." *Think, man. Think of an actual reason. One that doesn't involve you having to own up to the fact you've got a thing for the woman he wants you to protect!* "My boss has stood me down for the moment. I need time to sort my head out." He'd all but choked on those words, though somehow they'd spilled from his tongue easier than admitting to kissing Izzie had.

Jeez. He was so screwed.

A tapping came down the line and he caught the tail end of a sigh. "Ethan, I wouldn't be asking this if I had another option handy. Give me a week? I can probably organise something else by then, but Izzie knows my team here. I need an outside resource and you're one of the few people I trust. I served with your dad, and he was the best. I know you're cut from that same cloth."

Oh, man. Did he have to appeal to that side of him?

"I'm taking leave from work. My last job ... something went wrong, and it's messed with me." He swallowed at the pit of frustration broiling inside him. It killed him to admit that he had missed something, that he'd failed. He'd prefer to take a bullet a thousand times over than to have failed. "I screwed up."

Again with the pause.

"You didn't screw up. Look, I have some information for you. I'll forward it through. But you didn't screw up. You need a break though. You're working too hard."

Despair quickly swapped to confusion, then a sinking feeling of being played. Just what did Ian know that he didn't? "What the hell do you mean by all that?"

"I asked your boss to give you the time off. I thought Izzie was coming to Australia."

"So you had my boss order me to take leave?" His teeth gritted, anger coursing through his veins. He wanted to hit something. "Why the hell can't you just come and get the princess yourself? If she's in some kind of trouble, that's your problem. I'm not cleared for that."

"She's not in trouble from someone else."

"Then what is she running from?"

"Herself. I think." Ian's voice drooped, and Ethan heard the sense of helplessness in the other man's voice. It was odd, coming from someone he'd only ever heard at full strength. At least he wasn't the only one who'd seemed to fall under Izzie's spell. "I don't know. That's the problem. She's been erratic and there are other signs. Have you noticed anything? When you were with her today?"

Ethan paused, his mouth open, but the words didn't

come. Izzie had had the first stages of a panic attack. He'd seen it in her eyes, had felt it in her trembling body. But he'd also seen the scared look of a deer about to flee. She wasn't ready to talk about whatever was causing her issues. He'd seen that expression before on a fellow army mate after they'd been discharged. They'd both got out after serving in Iraq, but unlike his friend, he'd been left with only a few terrible memories. His friend had walked away haunted.

Izzie had had that same look.

That memory crushed the last of his resolve. Hadn't he known from the moment that Izzie had crumbled, that even without Ian's call he wasn't going anywhere? She might not want to talk to her family, but she needed to talk to someone. He couldn't desert her knowing how close to the edge she was.

"Nothing specific," he eventually said in response to Ian's question. "What did you mean earlier when you mentioned her issues were with her dad?"

He didn't bother to comment on the fact that Ian had included him in that category. It wasn't true.

"They aren't on great terms. There's a bit of a wall that's building between them. It's been mounting since the queen's death. Izzie is the spitting image of her mother. The king ... well he has said nothing, but I know he's hurting."

"You're on the king's detail?"

"No. I'm Izzie's bodyguard." The other man's tone was flat.

Ethan held back a curse. No wonder Ian was desperately searching for someone he could place his full trust in. "Does her father know where she is?"

"No. He's aware she's taken off, but I wanted to ensure her ongoing safety until I brief him. I fully intend to recommend he just let her be. Forcing her hand in coming home isn't what she needs right now. She needs someone she can talk to."

His heart beat a solid thump that reverberated through his body, through his skull. "Okay." One word that sealed his fate.

"I don't want payment," he said after another beat.

The pause was thick with recriminations, mainly from his own mind. His eyes slammed shut. Ian would surely make his own assumptions around that sentence.

"I see." The warmth from the other man's voice was all but gone. "Am I asking too much?"

God. Is he? He oscillated between admitting the truth and just saying he was already in too deep. Izzie's translucent face and wide blue eyes ripped into his mind. Even if he was in too deep and involved, it didn't matter now. He couldn't walk away from helping her in any way he could. "No. You can count on me. The job always comes first."

"That's an interesting motto."

"It was my father's."

Ian sighed down the line, could almost hear him open his mouth to speak, then close it a few times. "I grew up with your father and worked with him many times. I'm not sure I ever heard him use that as a motto. Do you ever talk to your mother about what happened to your father?"

What? "Where are you going with this, Ian?" Sudden frustration swamped him and he couldn't wait to get off the phone. "Never mind. I gotta go. I'll call this number if I have anything to update." Not waiting for a response, he ended the call.

He'd had enough flung onto his plate today. Over the years, his mother had tried to talk to him about his dad's death many times, but it was pointless. He knew what had happened. His dad had died from a gunshot wound he'd sustained doing his job. A job he'd loved and taken immense pride in. A job he'd put first.

His dad was a hero and had died a hero.

Ethan would be lucky if he could live up to even one tenth of his legacy.

7

———

The next day, Izzie stood under the steaming jets of the shower hoping it would wash away her intense confusion. Ethan had backed away. She'd all but seen the decision in his eyes to run, but then he'd shown up again, just as she'd needed him. Did the guy have telepathy?

And that kiss.

Neither had mentioned it. The taxi had delivered her to her front gate, and Izzie had been too scared to say anything. She'd bolted, and Ethan had let her go, wordlessly. Space was a welcome respite. At least until she could work out exactly what she should do next.

An enormous part of her ached to find Ethan and tell him the truth, to see how he reacted and whether it would even matter to him. Except that was throwing them both right into the deep end. Alternatively, she could just see where this casual attraction led them. But what if she ended up wanting more? Ethan already seemed to understand her on a level that no other man had gone to. What if she fell for him and then he left her when he found out the truth?

Was she really considering the L word after two days?

No. That was ludicrous. She was letting her emotional state run away from her. What she needed was to calm her mind, body and spirit. Yoga. It was the perfect answer.

After pulling on jet-black leggings and some thick cable-knit socks, she threw on a matching oversized cable-knit jumper. She snuggled into the wool, enjoying the warmth and familiar smell. She brushed out her hair and then wove it into a loose plait that fell halfway down her back. Tendrils floated forwards, but she quickly hooked them behind her ears.

Settling into a comfortable position on the carpet, she took a few deep breaths, hoping to calm her mind before she started her session. Except her mind refused to play along. Soft green eyes floated into her concentration, taunting her with their gaze that saw too much.

She shook her head. Enough breathing exercises—she'd just jump straight into a few sun salutations. Raising her arms high, she stretched out her back before carving her hands through the air and towards the floor. Exhale. Her eyes fluttered closed, focusing on the movements within her body, each muscle shifting into a familiar pattern and routine. A grin flashed. White teeth with a tiny chip on the front tooth that she'd felt with her tongue forced her eyes back into a wide-open stance.

Why the hell couldn't she concentrate?

A beep sounded from her bag. Her butt crashed to the carpeted floor, and she flopped into a spread-eagled pose. This was useless. Her mind refused to obey her commands to not think of Ethan and the kiss they'd shared.

After swinging to her side, she padded over to her bag and riffled through it until she found the familiar silver sparkle cover of her phone. Turning it over, she sighed. Felix wasn't giving up easily.

Huffing at the injustice, she dialled his number, surprised that it connected after one short ring.

"Where the hell are you?"

"Hi to you too."

"We've been worried sick, Izzie."

"Excuse me. Just because you're suddenly settled—have you forgotten how often you pulled a disappearing act in the past few years?"

"No, I haven't forgotten. But nor did I ever neglect to mention to *someone* where I was going. You vanished."

"Apparently not well enough. How did you find me?"

"You used your debit card."

Izzie frowned. She'd used her fake-name debit card. how the hell—

"The one I helped you set up when you were eighteen?" Her brother inserted just as her memories clicked into place.

"Dammit," she muttered. "Have you told anyone else?"

"Not yet. I wanted to talk to you first, but Dad's been beside himself. He said you two argued."

Izzie's heart skipped. He'd spoken about that?

"Some argument over the international relations position. He told me he wanted me to take it, but honestly if it means this much to you, I'll tell him no."

Air whooshed out of Izzie's lungs in one giant puff. *Different argument.* "You should take it. It will mean travel all over. You and Sophia could see the world."

"I don't need to see the world. That's your dream. So the job is why you've run away?"

She zeroed in on his last two words, which hurt. But then the truth always did. And she *was* running. Though not just because of the job. Izzie was running from herself, and so far she hadn't even done a suitable job of that. She'd hoped to find a clarity, space to set her mind in the right direction so she could find her way again. So far everything she did just turned into a mess.

"I really want that job, yes. I always have. That's what I studied for. It's what Mum, Dad and I always discussed." Izzie was proud of herself for only fumbling slightly over her use of the term mum.

"Dad will come around. He's just worried that you're flighty. Come home. Prove him wrong. We all know you can."

Except they were wrong.

"That's just it. *I'm* not sure I can." She hung up.

Anytime she faced her past, it all flung back at warp speeds and sent her into a tumbling mess of panic. Her heart palpitations were so loud, she wondered at the noise before being able to place her response—she'd admitted something truthful. She'd opened up a paltry amount. How long had it been since that happened?

Her phone rang again. Expecting to see Felix's number, she raised her brows as Ethan's flashed on the screen. Her heart rate changed its tune, slowing to a different beat, one of excitement.

She smiled as she connected the call. "Hey."

"Hey, yourself. I'm thinking we need to find a fresh challenge—one that won't leave me crippled and looking like a fool."

She giggled. "Ice skating isn't for the faint-hearted." Relief that he'd reached out to her and all seemed to be normal flooded her. Maybe he'd also been thrown by the kiss and just needed time out to sort through it. "What did you have in mind?"

"You'll find out in the morning. Be ready by eight."

"Do I get a dress code at least?"

"Dress for the Arctic Circle."

She frowned, pulling her lips to the side in thought. The line went dead before she could question him any further. Instead of waiting for the inevitable next call from her brother, she switched off the phone. It was time to finish her yoga. Her mind now seemed far more accommodating.

———

"When you said Arctic Circle, I thought maybe some cool breakfast cafe that featured ice sculpture furniture."

"Really?" Ethan dead-panned. He'd thought that telling her to dress warm would have been a giveaway for this next adventure, and it sure promised to be a fun one. They'd been briefed on the safety instructions and given life jackets to wear. Ethan had his ski jacket on which was waterproof, but he worried about Izzie's jacket. It definitely looked warm but he couldn't be sure on the waterproof factor. "Will you be warm enough in that? It gets freezing out on the water."

"Well, I guess we'll find out," she replied with a lopsided grin which turned mischievous. "You might have to cuddle me to keep me extra warm."

Internally, he groaned. Thoughts of holding her in his arms and kissing her again had invaded his dreams all night long. But between them sat lies—a great big fat one on both of their behalves. She wasn't being honest about who she was, and now, nor was he. She'd asked him outright if he was on a job. He'd said no, but those lines had definitely blurred since then. He was on a protection service now —hers.

He was saved from commenting by one of the Shotover Jet boat crew coming forward to explain a few extra safety instructions and complete a general health check. Ethan shrugged his shoulder, rotating the muscle around a little. He'd gone for a punishing run again this morning, even when his body had screamed at the torment after yesterday's unathletic ice display. He'd taken this boat ride before so knew that he was in for a series of supersonic speedy twists and turns, and his body being flung about. They checked for any current injuries. Last time he'd taken this trip, he'd been injury free, but he figured he'd tough out this one.

He needed to spend time with Izzie, to delve further into what was going on in that delectable mind of hers without giving himself away. And unfortunately without giving in to his growing need to kiss her again. A promise he'd made to himself that was far easier when declared in front of the mirror, but not as much when the five-foot six package stood before him. She glanced at him from the corner of her eye, throwing him a cheeky wink.

At least she seemed to be back in better spirits today. At the rink, he was certain he'd gotten a glimpse of the real Izzie, but today was he was getting the show? Bright and bubbly, all wrapped up in the always-present elegant package. He hated himself for missing her depths from the day before. He missed the raw honesty he'd witnessed on her face.

It was that girl who called to him.

They were ushered down steep steps towards a pontoon where they'd board the boat.

"What made you think of this as an activity?"

"I've done it before. Figured it might fit your need for adventure and fast fun."

"What makes you think I'm into action adventure?"

"Your enjoyment of strapping razor-thin blades onto your feet and dancing on ice for one."

"Ha! So from ice skating, you thought I'd like to fly around on a jet boat aimed at canyons?"

"They aren't always aiming at the canyons."

She shook her head at him, and he caught a slight eye-roll. Her hair was sliding out of its bun and she reached up, pulling it out and allowing it to tumble about her face in a golden cascade. The sun glinted off strands and he itched to reach out and wrap a piece around his finger. Before he could shift, she flung it back using both her hands and then gathered it into a loose plait. In a move she'd probably done millions of times, she brought the plait to the side of her neck and tucked it under her collar. It was artless—an action so practised, she probably didn't even think twice about it, but it left him a little dazed.

"Do you want my beanie?" he offered.

Another jet came careening around from the left, almost hovering across the water, such was its speed. Water flung in its wake as it performed a tight donut turn and then continued to race in its original direction. He noted Izzie's mouth drop open a little, her gaze tracking the fast-disappearing signature red boat.

"I'm not sure I can guarantee its safe return," she said with a grimace.

He shrugged, though she didn't see. He pulled the beanie from his back pocket and wordlessly held it towards her. It wasn't anything expensive, but it might help provide a little more warmth for her. His lips twitched a little when he saw she still wore his possum gloves from the day before.

Her fingers brushed against his—on purpose, he was sure—as she took the piece of wool from his hand. He blocked the mild tingle her touch had left, balling his hand into a fist and shoving it into his jacket pocket. Hell, he hadn't even connected with her skin. He needed to rein in these feelings, and fast. He couldn't afford another balls-up around a job—even if this was wasn't officially on the books.

His mouth tightened, the frustration at being put on leave still rife.

"If it pains you that much, I'm really happy to skip wearing it." Blue eyes that held amusement and a little confusion blinked at him.

"Sorry?"

"You frowned, after handing over the beanie." She hadn't put it on her head. Her fingers folded and unfolded the fabric, turning it around in her hands.

"Not related. I was thinking about work." Why had he admitted that?

"You aren't the only wonderful listener," she offered. Her lips shifted into that brief half smile he noted she did whenever she was a little unsure of herself. Just how did someone like her appear to have self-esteem issues? Was this the real Princess Isabella? Showing her true colours because she thought she was a complete unknown?

He'd spent a few hours last night doing some homework and reading through the information that Ian had sent through to him. That picture painted a young, carefree and confident woman, if not perhaps a little vapid and shallow. There was nothing of the uncertainty he'd seen in her smile or shadows in her eyes since they'd been spending time together.

Either way, he planned to unearth what had brought her halfway around the world and into his orbit. "Let's save anymore heart to hearts for later. I think we might find talking a little difficult soon."

They moved forward as the group were finally led down to the boat, having been cleared to board and get clipped in. Ethan could feel Izzie's jittery excitement in the vibrations she was giving off. At least he hoped it was excitement—her head was cast down as she took a tentative step into the boat and shuffled across to the far side, leaving room for him.

"Let's swap," he said. After twisting so she could shift back across one seat, he took the outer side, closest to the water.

"Why? I'm not about to jump off the side."

"That thought hadn't crossed my mind. But I think I'll handle the water in the face a little better."

That earned him an arched brow and mocking smile. "Like that, is it, macho boy?"

He chuckled, but was quickly distracted by how she snuggled in against his side. He really hoped this would not end with her getting pneumonia. He pulled his safety harness tight, checking that Izzie's was also locked in, which earned him another look.

The jet engine roared to life and any more chat became impossible. The boat swung in a wide arc, and then the driver gunned the throttle and they flew off down the river. The air whipped against his cheeks, instantly chilling him. He heard a slight squeak from beside him. Tilting his head an inch, he looked at Izzie, taking care not to turn too much in case the speed flung his glasses off.

Her smile was something else and his heart did a funny wobble. Though he attributed it to the sudden turn, as the boat felt like it all but tipped 90 degrees on its side and aimed directly at a sheer rock face. Muffled squeals mixed with other shouts of excitement bounced about as the boat dipped again at the last minute and zipped past the rock with what appeared to be millimetres to spare.

They flew along the river, the momentum throwing them around a little. Ethan allowed a smile of exhilaration to cross his mouth. Damn, he'd forgotten how much fun this was. Without warning, they dived into a turn that had the boat spinning almost on the spot, creating a huge splash that Ethan copped. He hissed and spluttered, the water so cold, it was as if shards of ice had pierced his skin.

The boat idled as the driver called out to check everyone was okay. His smug expression gave the impression this was part of the experience. Ethan shook his head to rid his face of some remaining droplets.

Izzie's head leaned in close against his, her nose touching his cheek briefly. It was as cold as the water had been. "Thanks for swapping."

He turned to her, their noses almost brushing. The warm air of her exhale hit his cheek. Looking deep into those eyes that sparkled with fun and life, he lost his train of thought, forgetting what he'd been going to say. There was that expression again—gone were any signs of the haunted secrets from the day before. Nor was there any of the glazed disinterest so common in all the public photos he'd flicked through the previous night. It was the same look he'd seen in her eyes when she'd been lost in her ice skating. And after he'd kissed her.

He swallowed, his chest tight. The boat took off again, and he was thankful for the distraction.

A fuzzy finger brushed across his hand and then slid in to grip his hand. The rest of the trip was a blur of movement as he tried to keep his focus on the activity and not how good it was to be holding Izzie's hand.

He was in serious trouble.

8

$\mathcal{E}$than flexed his shoulder, rolling it around to loosen up the muscles. Yesterday had been more fun than he'd expected, and after the jet boat ride, he and Izzie had spent the rest of the day hanging out.

It had never been this easy to just hang out and pass time with a woman.

He'd surprised himself this morning when he'd woken —his plans for going skiing dull compared to the excitement he'd felt at seeing Izzie's face again, and hearing her laugh. Plus, it was his job to monitor her, and he never shirked on any of his work. He'd tossed aside skiing and called, inviting her to lunch. At least he hadn't begged her to meet him earlier as he'd initially been tempted to do..

You are so toast.

Slamming his eyes shut to block out his unwanted thoughts, he caught the gentle floral tones of Izzie's perfume before cool fingers crept into place over his eyes.

"Guess who?"

"Goldilocks."

She laughed, as he'd hoped. Collecting her fingers, he

pulled them away before spinning to face her. Even though he'd told himself to be cool, his breath hitched at the sight of her. She'd left her hair out. The long, wavy locks fell over her shoulder, shining with the appearance of silk. She wore jeans with a high-necked top tucked in, emphasising her tiny waist. Her boots came over her knees and he had to hold in a groan. The cheeky glint in her eye told him his perusal hadn't gone unnoticed.

He cleared his throat. "So, uh, what do you feel like for lunch?"

"I figured you'd have that worked out, since you invited me."

"Right. Yep. How do you feel about burgers? There's an awesome place a few blocks over from here."

"I have a lot of time for burgers. So long as there's also chips and bacon."

"Bacon?"

"Yep. It's not a burger without bacon." She grabbed his hand as they walked, swinging it with a bubbly happiness.

He whistled, shaking his head. "You're something else, Isabella."

Her arm twitched, and a sideways glance showed him her smile dimming a little. "Let's stick with Izzie. I prefer it."

"Okay." *Interesting.* "So do you plan to go skiing at all whilst you're here?"

"Probably not."

"All this way for some of the best snow around and you're not even going to ski? Surely you know what you're doing, with your balance and all."

"No. I just ... skiing kind of has connotations that I'd prefer to not revisit. Not today anyway."

He nodded, keeping quiet. They walked the rest of the

way in silence. Izzie was lost in her thoughts, and he was left in the company of his own.

They ordered, then grabbed one booth along the wall. Inside it was cosy, and he struggled not to admire Izzie's slim figured as she stripped off her overcoat. In the high boots and black top, she looked like she'd just walked off the set of *Charlie's Angels*. That was the vibe he was getting from her—that she was ready to slay any baddies who stepped into her path. Except his intuition told him she didn't have any baddies in her life, just demons in her mind.

She twisted a ring on her finger, around and around. "The last holiday I went on with my mum was a ski trip."

He leaned in to hear her soft words better, leaving her to continue.

"It was wonderful." A slight smile tugged at the corner of her mouth, but it held a world of sadness. He couldn't see her eyes. They were trained to the table.

Silence stretched as he waited for her to add anything more.

"You miss her," he said.

"Every moment of every day. I wish ... anyway, it doesn't matter now."

"You were very close?"

"Aren't all kids close with their mums?" She deflected with a smile that didn't reach her eyes. "I love this song! Gosh, I haven't heard it in forever."

He tried to pick up the lyrics—something about staying together and being in love—but his mind wasn't on task. He was still trying to read what was really going on with Izzie. Ian had implied she had issues with her father, but it seemed more likely that her issues were stemming from the loss of her mother.

She started humming along and then broke out into

song. The place was packed and noisy, but her voice carried out across the crowd, drawing a few admiring eyes. It was the voice of an angel. He could only shake his head in wonder. She was full of surprises. Her body moved in a smooth and hypotonic rhythm. He bet she'd look amazing out on a dance floor—the sort of dancer who would really throw her all into the task. Even knowing he couldn't dance to save his life, he mentally added taking her dancing to his list.

As the song ended, there was a round of applause and she giggled, pleased by the attention. It was a side of her he hadn't seen yet. But he was learning that only time would tell if it was part of the real Izzie.

Their burgers were delivered, and they both dived in with gusto. Ethan groaned as the juicy flavour of pork, spiced tomato and garlic hit his taste buds.

"You like to sing?" he asked around his next bite.

"Not as much as you like burgers," she replied with a giant grin. "But yeah, I love to sing. Sorry—I should've warned you I'm prone to breaking out into song when the mood strikes."

"Don't apologise. You have an amazing voice."

She raised a brow in disbelief. "I think amazing is a bit of a stretch. We should totally find a karaoke bar though—wouldn't that be fun!"

About as much as sticking needles into my eyes. "Yeah sure, why not?"

Her laugh was loud, drawing a few gazes again. There it was again—the different Izzie. Brighter. Lighter. Infecting others with happiness. "You're a terrible liar."

He shoved the last of his burger into his mouth, choosing not to reply. His mother had always taught him not to disagree with a woman when she was correct. Picking up a napkin, he wiped a bit of sticky residue from his fingers. Izzie reached out to grab a napkin, her fingers brushing against his, causing tingles to shoot up his arms.

This was feeling like a date. He needed to put some space between them and find his perspective. He was— unofficially and unpaid—working. That needed to be front and centre in his mind. "Excuse me a moment. I just gotta go to the bathroom."

Having just taken a giant bite of her own burger, she gave him a wave with her free hand.

The chair scraped as he pushed to stand and strode towards the toilets. Not needing to go, he instead leaned against the mirrored sink and looked his reflection in the eye. He didn't dare speak. It wouldn't do to be caught talking to himself in the bathroom, but he gave himself a stern mental lecture.

Get a grip, man. You're acting like a putz. Time to get your head back in the game and focus on your task.

He washed his hands, taking his time, not wanting to return to the table too quickly. When he got back, he was surprised to find Izzie had finished her burger and was on the phone.

His phone.

"Barbara, just a moment, Ethan's back. I'd better pass you over before I get in trouble."

He couldn't hear his mother's response, but it made Izzie laugh and her eyes shine with mirth before she silently handed the phone to him.

"Mum?"

"Darling. I was just calling to check in. You hadn't told me you'd met someone over there. Now I understand why you haven't been skiing yet."

He scrunched his eyes tight, rubbing at his temple. His

mother would take two and two and come up with twelve. Why had he admitted to her yesterday that he hadn't skied yet? "It's not …" He caught the slight lift of Izzie's brow and changed direction. "Was there something you needed, Ma?"

"Can't a mum just want to chat to her favourite boy?"

"I'm your only boy, and I'm on holiday, remember?"

"Is that your not-so-subtle way of telling me to mind my beeswax?"

"Yes."

"Ha! Fine. Put Isabella back on."

"Mum …"

"Ethan Doran Raines, do not take that tone with me."

He gave up, instead handing the phone over in silence.

"Hi again, Barbara." There was the laugh. "Yeah, he's frowning all right."

He wiped all expression from his face, ignoring the smirk that earned him from Izzie.

The two women chatted for a while longer before Izzie rang off. She placed the phone in front of him.

"Sorry. Your phone rang, and I might have noticed the screen said Mum so I just answered. I know you said your mum likes to check in on you and I didn't want her to worry." Her voice was a little meek.

"I'm not angry. My mother is a force to be reckoned with. Actually, I should thank you for answering, otherwise she would have started on the hospitals."

"She's amazing."

"She's nosy. Needs to find a hobby that isn't monitoring my life or baking cakes."

Izzie stood and leaned in, placing a whisper-soft kiss against his cheek. "Don't take it for granted. You're lucky to have someone who loves you that much." She straightened, an odd look on her face. "Should we go get ice cream?"

Ethan's head spun. He had a belly full of burger and chips along with having witnessed a surreal yet happy conversation between his mum and a runaway princess ... Now she wanted ice cream? Where the hell did she put all the food she ate?

"Your wish is my command," he answered.

"I wish." Her wink was pure seductress.

Yep. Toast.

"So tell me more about Izzie. I know skiing isn't a chief priority, though I'd still love to change your mind on that. You were a professional ice skater in a previous life. Which leads me to think you're really into winter?"

She smiled at Ethan's assessment. It was sweet and honest given what he knew about her from this trip, but it was also far from the truth. At least the truth of the past five years. She'd used to be a real winter baby ... Just when had she made that change to do nothing but chase the sun?

Mum's death.

The thought was unwelcome, but unfortunately true.

"Actually, more recently I've been known to always chase the sun. That's why I came here."

"For something different?" Ethan queried.

"No. Because I figured this would be one of the last places they'd look for me." She let out a soft laugh.

Ethan's hand reached out, and his fingers brushed her thigh. "Are you running away from someone?"

It took her a moment to for his words to register—she was so swept up in her own realisation of how she'd unknowingly been running from winter. She halted, her eyes flying to his in panic.

"Uh. No. I didn't mean it like that."

She struggled to hold his gaze. His was full of warmth and an invitation to share, to be honest. But could she?

No.

"Did I say that? I just meant that this was out of character for me. Wanting to chase something different. The last place my thoughts would catch me."

"Are your thoughts such an issue?"

God, she was hot. Swallowing was a struggle, as was breathing. Why wouldn't he stop looking at her like that? Like she was an insect under a microscope. "I'm twenty-eight. Surely it's time for me to escape my thoughts for a little while."

"So you weren't referring to your dad? And the family business?"

She stilled, his words trapping her as effectively as a noose. "Well. My career is tied up in my thoughts, yes. But I didn't mean them specifically." Okay, that was a lie. Well, sort of. She didn't want them to find her.

But more than anything, she didn't want any part of her current life to catch up to her here until she could sort out what was holding her back from her future. Hell. She was a princess of a small European country. She was richer than any person needed to be. Money was of no consequence. And still she couldn't settle into anything.

Her desire for the international relations job wasn't even really there anymore, and that scared her. That had been one of the last sure things she had any form of clarity on from before her mother died.

No. Before her mother had taken her own life.

That distinction had her doubling over in pain.

How dare she!

"Izzie?" Ethan's voice was at her ear. He crouched beside

her bent form, his eyes pools of concern that she wanted to dive into, to lose herself in and never come back up for air.

But it wasn't an option.

She would never be that … that one word.

Weak.

"I'm fine."

"Are you?"

She looked at the knit collar of the jumper he wore beneath his ski jacket. It was the closest she could get to his face without wanting to cringe in embarrassment. Not moments ago, they'd been laughing and chatting to his mum.

Straightening her legs, she shifted back to a standing position. "I'm getting there."

"Do you want to talk about it?"

"Not right now. But someday, yes. I think I want to talk to you. About it."

"Name the day and I'm yours."

The double meaning there had her smiling. If only because she could see in his eyes that his words were pure and true, no entendre intended. Had she ever met anyone as honest as Ethan Raines?

"Can we rain check our plans for this afternoon? I think I need to go do yoga."

His brow quirked. "Yoga?"

"Yeah. It's calming. You should try it sometime."

"All right. The day you need to talk, we'll talk, then we'll do yoga."

"Ha! That almost makes me want to talk. Almost."

His arms wrapped around her, cocooning her with warmth and a feeling of utmost safety. The hug was nothing short of divine, leaving a soft smile on her face for the duration of her walk back to her accommodation.

She could only wish it would last.

After closing the door behind her with a quiet click, she dropped her bag onto the side table and the keys into the handy bowl provided. A quick glance in the hallway mirror showed a stranger—eyes strangely wide and darting about the place, her complexion pale. Hair that had fussed into frizz town from too much handling and flicking behind her ears. She looked—scared. Turning away from the unfavourable view, she walked into the bedroom and changed into her yoga gear. After flicking on the heater, she sat on the ground, her legs stretched out before her as she turned her thoughts to her breathing. Her eyes closed. Her hearing sharpened, soaking in all the surrounding sounds.

She could hear the heater's slight clunk as it repositioned its airflow, and a bird chirruping from outside in the small courtyard. Turning her focus inwards, she dragged in a deep breath, trying to fill every part of herself possible, then let it out with a whoosh. After repeating the movement a few times, she had calmed her mind enough to turn her thoughts back to the awful night.

Memories assaulted her.

A conversation with her mother. Her mum talking about how she wished she were more like her daughter, more like Izzie. *If only I wasn't so weak.* Had her mum really said those words?

Izzie had been heading out to a nightclub, meeting her beau of the moment. Goodness, she couldn't even remember the guy's name. They'd argued, her mum telling her he wasn't for her. He'd ended up being a total looser and had spent the night talking non-stop about himself. Some investment banker slash lord from London. She'd endured it by drinking way too much. But before she'd left, before she'd argued with her mum, Izzie had been excited. Bubbling with happiness—that was what her mum had said—like a tall glass of champagne. Why had her mum wanted to be more like her?

Think, Izzie. Think.

Her mother had said she was tired, exhausted of all the parties and events. Too many late nights and ... *not enough time to just sit and breath*. Had her mother been trying to tell her something then?

Was that why she hadn't been able to remember this before? Was that what all the panic attacks were about? Were her thoughts revolting within her body, warning her they were about to explode forth like a volcano, ready to cover her in hot, fiery lava and burn her alive?

Her stomach swirled, threatening its own eruption. As if her body was trying to rid itself of her thoughts and memories in any way it could.

Had her mother seemed tired? Distracted? Izzie had been wrapped up in her own thoughts and hadn't been paying proper attention. What if she'd stayed in that night? What if she'd been less self-absorbed and had just stayed ... Would she have been able to stop her mother? What if she hadn't argued with her about going out?

No. She'd been through this journey a million times. Hell, she wasn't the only one. Hadn't her brother, Henrik, admitted his own guilt and thoughts of what if—blaming himself for not being able to stop their mother's suicide? She'd accepted a long time ago that what her mother had done, she'd done from a place of pure unhappiness and mental health issues. She'd chosen to take her life. She'd chosen to stop her medication and had walked away from her family.

The thought still swept Izzie's breath away, creating a

hurt so deep that her grip on reality swirled in darkness. Who took their own life?

No. That wasn't the problem.

The problem was still buried there ... deep down.

Izzie might hate herself for being one of the last people to see her mother alive. She definitely hated herself for being the first person to find her mum dead. But no one could ever hate her more than her father, who had laid the whole sorry mess at her feet. And who still blamed her to this day, even though there was nothing Izzie could have done to save her mother.

That was the problem.

9
———

"You know, you still haven't told me your last name."

Izzie startled over Ethan's question. They were walking along the lake's edge, eating ice cream, as had become a bit of a daily ritual.

"Um, really? I'm sure we would have covered that," she murmured, buying herself some time. She was well aware she hadn't shared her last name, or any further personal details with him, instead keeping it light and blocking any reminders of her actual life from her mind. Which had left her feeling somewhat better, if not a definite sense of being in denial.

They'd spent the past week hanging out every moment of the day, and sometimes late into the night. It had been the perfect escape, and for the first time in ages, she could breathe easy. Her only gripe was that Ethan was keeping his distance. Every step she made to deepen their connection, he sidestepped.

She couldn't quite find her footing with Ethan. He liked her—that was obvious. And the desire she sometimes caught shining in his eyes when he thought she wasn't looking definitely told her he was interested in her physically. And yet ... not once had he made a move to kiss her again. If she had to put money on it, she'd say he was avoiding touching her altogether.

But, why?

"Izzie?"

"Huh?"

"You haven't told me your last name."

"Oh!" Crap. They were still on this. She'd totally spaced. "Correll."

"Isabella Correll," he repeated. A funny look shifted across his features before it disappeared.

"Ethan Raines," she replied with a smile.

"That's an interesting last name."

She shrugged, searching for some way to change the subject. And fast. Correll had been her mother's maiden name and the name used on her passport. Well, her fake passport. So for now—that's exactly who Ethan Raines was with. No way did she want Ethan to have any chance of connecting her with Princess Isabella Steninska of Stenaco.

A part of her urged her to tell the truth, to open up fully, but she wasn't ready. They'd known each other such a short time, she didn't want to ruin what they had with the truth. They passed a car with skis strapped to the roof racks, snow still stuck within the bindings.

"You haven't gone skiing yet," she blurted.

"Guess I've been distracted." He licked at his chocolate cone and Izzie had the urge to swipe her finger across the ice cream where his mouth had just been. His eyes flicked sideways, tiny crinkles at the corners showing his amusement. "I'd be happy to go tomorrow though, if you're keen?"

"Sure. Why not? Guess that means this afternoon must be my turn to organise an activity?"

Ethan chuckled. "That shouldn't make me scared, but somehow, it does."

"Oh, come on. The luge was fun. The ice bar, perhaps, not as good an idea."

"At least the drinks were chilly."

"True. Especially when spilled all over your lap."

A bike cycled towards them, flying along, the rider on the phone. Ethan's arm grabbed her about the waist and quickly shuffled her to his other side. The bike zoomed past, giving them a wide berth, but Ethan's manoeuvre left her with a slight grin. "Ever the hero?"

His arm that had still been holding her side dropped away. "Something like that."

"Tell me more about being a bodyguard. What sort of jobs do you normally take on?"

"Mainly security detail for the rich and powerful. Sometimes other work—surveillance."

"Okay, Mr Vague. Enlighten me about your last job."

If she hadn't been looking directly at his face, she would have missed the grimace that flashed across his mouth. "It should have been routine. A business man was in final negotiations for launching some tech product that would get the company out of trouble. He'd been worried someone was following him and just wanted a little safety insurance. My role was to accompany him to the meeting. On the drive there, the car stalled, which I should have realised was a sign things were about to go pear-shaped. Next thing I know, there are sniper bullets ricocheting about the place. I caught one in the shoulder."

"You were shot! That's what you call a routine job?"

"No. That job ..." He rubbed a hand across his jaw,

anguish pulling his eyebrows together. "... anyway. The deal went through."

"What were you about to say?"

He paused for a moment, tugging her arm and then leading her along a path to the sandy area surrounding the lake. He took the last bite of his cone, chewing in silence as if buying himself time. He balled the napkin in his hand and then shoved both into his jeans pockets. Wind ruffled his hair. She wanted to reach out and run her fingers through his fringe, which was flopping to the left a little.

"Something about the job has never sat right with me. He was shot. Died on the scene."

Izzie gasped. "That's terrible. Is that why you're on leave?"

His eyes swung to hers, locking on and looking deeply, as if he were trying to read her soul. "In a roundabout way, yes. I wouldn't leave it alone. My boss told me to take it easy with my shoulder healing, but I just couldn't shake the idea that I'd missed something."

"Like what?"

"Like why hire a sniper over a business deal? It wasn't even that big a deal. The shooter was 1500 metres away, which means they were good. Expert." His eyes drifted, glancing out across the water as though hoping for answers from its inky surface.

"Maybe it wasn't about the deal."

Ethan frowned. "What do you mean?"

"Well, maybe it was someone else. Is he married? Maybe his wife wanted to get rid of him. Isn't that the most common link—unhappy spouses or family members?" Izzie let out a laugh. She wasn't really being serious, but had hoped it might lighten the mood a little.

Ethan had missed the memo though—he was looking at

her with an intense scrutiny that caused a shiver along her spine. "The wife was never questioned. Hell, we never even thought to look at her."

His movements were rigid. Gone was the relaxed mood of before, replaced by an energy that floated around him.

"Do you need to go?" she asked.

He looked at her. "Would you mind?"

"No. You should go make some calls. I know what it's like to have something eating away at you. I'll put my time to expert use, finding us something to do tomorrow."

"I mightn't be that long ..."

"It's fine. Really. I'm getting sick of you, anyway." She grinned, which turned to surprise when he leaned in and smacked a kiss straight on her lips.

"You are amazing." His words warmed her almost as much as the kiss had.

He jogged back onto the path and towards where they were both staying.

At least one of them had seemed to find some answers. Izzie was still a long way from finding any clarity in her life, but she was breathing easier. And if she just kept avoiding any memories of her mother, and thoughts of her father's blame, the panic attacks would stay away.

Izzie had been enjoying her freedom, but if she didn't turn her phone on at least once a day to message Felix, he'd probably send out the Stenish National Guard. Which would be quite the sight in downtown Queenstown.

She nursed a coffee. After taking a fortifying sip of the hot, bitter liquid, she let it slide down her throat before pressing the button at the base of her phone to bring it back to life.

Funny. Before she'd come on this trip, she wouldn't have been caught dead with her phone switched off. She would have been regularly scouring social media for mentions of her, checking what damage control was required or what she'd be reprimanded over next.

A part of her missed that connection, missed knowing what others were doing, what was trending, but she couldn't deny that just being plain old Isabella Correll was really growing on her. She'd even stopped looking over her shoulder, searching for unwanted cameras aimed her way, or scrutinising passers-by in case they'd been hired to follow her.

Felix had sworn that so long as she checked in with him daily, he wouldn't breathe a word of her location.

She wasn't deluded—her time here wasn't endless, but she'd fight for every skerrick of time with Ethan she could until she had to own up to the inevitable bombshell of truth.

Her phone blinked to life, a stream of messages from Felix appearing on the screen.

She clicked *dial* to call him, figuring it would be easier for him to just fill her in over the phone. "I was just talking about you."

"Hi to you too. Marvellous things I should hope?"

"I'm with Eva and Sophia. So yes."

"Oh." Izzie paused. "Uh, how are they?"

"Good. Plotting fashion domination for next month's summer twilight ball."

Izzie's heart skipped a beat. She'd completely forgotten all about that ball. How was it even possible she'd blanked such an event? It had been one of her yearly highlights for as long as she could remember ... That and Milan fashion week.

Felix continued, ignoring her silence. "Eva's wondering if she needs to add you into her schedule."

"What have you told them? About me?"

He sighed. Through the phone, she could hear him excuse himself. There was a clink and slight rattle, then added outside noises told her he'd probably moved outside to be alone.

"Nothing. They are worried about you, but I said you're fine—just needed some thinking space. Like me, they'd love to know exactly what you need the thinking space from. I know you mentioned the job the other day, but is that really all there is to this?"

Izzie swallowed, the hairs on her arms standing to attention as a cool wind suddenly whipped past. Except it wasn't just an outer chill, there was an inner one too. Her heartbeat quickened, bounding about like a squirrel shooting up a tree to safety. Her eyes slammed shut, and she tried to focus on just breathing. *In. Out. In.* Green eyes punctured her vision, their dazzling depths providing a straightforward path to a calm she'd never found before.

"No." The word was out before she could think it through. "There's more. A lot more. I'm just not ready to talk about it yet though."

"Okay. Thank you—for admitting that at least. You sound kind of different. Relaxed. Less ... bouncy."

"Must be the fresh air. I'm fine, really."

"I have your word that you'll contact me, should that change? Henrik spoke to Ian yesterday. He admitted you'd blacked out before the Summer Festival opening. Father told us you were drunk, but when Henrik questioned Ian about that he appeared surprised."

"I wasn't drunk."

"Is it something else? Are you … sick?"

"I'm not sick, no. And I know you guys have been watching me like a hawk, wondering if I'm suffering mental health issues like mum, but it's not that. I'm not depressed. I'm just … in a contemplation phase. I need to find my path again."

God. Had she just admitted that?

"I think I should talk to Dad about the job—"

"No. Felix. Just no."

"But you want it, and if that's what's keeping you away—"

"It's not. It might have been the catalyst that sent me running, but it's not why I'm still here. Felix, Dad's right. I'm not the best person for that job currently. I'm qualified, sure. But I need to sort out a few things in my head. I'd be a liability to the crown in that role currently. Maybe not in the way Dad thinks, but a liability nonetheless."

Muffled noises came down the line, a quiet expletive, and then Izzie caught the tail end of Henrik's voice issuing a demand to have the phone. "Jeez, Izz, can you stop talking in riddles? Just tell us what's wrong so we can help!"

"Hi, big brother, nice to hear your voice." It wasn't a lie. As much as she was grimacing at Felix's obvious betrayal of keeping their chat a secret, it felt good to hear Henrik's voice. Plus, it was nice he used plural terms. He'd always held himself up as a pillar of solitude, having to go it alone. Eva had been such a wonderful influence on him.

"Cut it out, Izzie. We're worried sick here. I had to threaten Felix to get him to talk."

"Please, no throwing punches. I'm fine. I'm sure Felix will fill you in on where I am. I'll be home for the ball.

Please tell your gorgeously talented wife I am in need of a gown, if she has time."

"The ball is over a month away. You're planning to be absent all that time?"

"Not planning, no. Look, I don't have concrete plans. I just know I'm not ready yet okay? But I'm fine. Perfectly safe. I've met someone. He's really ... different, but in a marvellous way. Love you both." She hung up before they could respond.

Her phone rang immediately, but she hit decline and switched the device off again. Easier to just return to radio silence.

She dragged in a deep breath and let it out again slowly.

Had that been another panic attack that had threatened? And if so, had thoughts of Ethan brushed it away as casually as one would a hair on their arm?

The thought befuddled her mind.

After paying for her coffee, she walked back to her tiny house, which was increasingly starting to feel like a very cosy—if not small—home. A sign caught her eye as she walked, and she paused her steps. The image had her lips pulling into a wide grin.

Now that definitely fit the bill for an activity she and Ethan could do tomorrow.

Ethan waited for the call to connect, his hand slapping his thigh in a rhythmic beat. Boundless energy coursed through his veins. Could it be that they'd missed something with the investigation?

They'd scoured this guy's files, spoken to his work associates, but turned up nil. Ethan's boss had eventually ruled he couldn't be involved anymore, said that it was hindering his recuperation. He'd been assigned desk work, which had only increased his urge to find out the truth.

But what if he had been looking in the wrong direction? Izzie's comment had clicked.

"Cameron speaking."

"Thank God, man. You're hard to get hold of."

"Yeah, life's been busy. Besides, aren't you meant to be on holiday? It's customary to avoid any contact with the office when one's on leave." Ethan could hear his mate's smirk down the line.

"Yeah, yeah. I've just thought of something. Or, well, Izzie did, but never mind that. What if it was the wife?"

"Huh? Don't tell me this is about the Thomson case again, man? You've gotta let it go."

"I can't. That was a routine job accompanying him to a board meeting because of new software. I ended up shot, and he ended up dead. I missed something. I know I did. The files weren't even touched! No one has made any move on them—no claims, nothing."

The sigh was heartfelt but also resigned. "All right. So what makes you think it was the wife?"

"I don't know. What about his personal financials? Did we ever get anything on that? The company was make or break on that software, but he still had the most to lose if the software was stolen. So it makes no sense unless it was unrelated. Maybe we've been focusing on the wrong area all this time."

"Dude. You got issues. But okay—if it will get you off this case and your head back into the game, then I'll check it out. But seriously, if this goes nowhere, do I have your word you're done? Strewth, man. You're in Queenstown. The snow can't be that crap!"

"I owe you one."

"Yeah, yeah," he said, then hung up.

Ethan tossed the phone onto the counter then walked outside to lean against the railing. The frigid air brushed his skin, and he breathed in deeply. *Finally.*

If it had been the wife, for whatever reason, that made sense. She had access to money—the family were stinking rich and lived in a mansion along the water, pristine views of the Harbour Bridge at their doorstep. But what if that life wasn't quite what it seemed? The client had taken his business to the edge over that software. The sale had been make or break. The others on the board had said it was all agreed upon and the money had all come from the company, but what if that wasn't the entire truth? If he'd been using his own money as well ... it would paint quite a different picture.

He shook his head, shaking off thoughts of the case that he hadn't been able to leave alone. This was the first time since he'd gone into private protection that a case hadn't crossed all the T's and dotted all the I's. He wasn't sure if it was the fact he'd gotten shot, or the image of his client's life fading in front of his eyes, but he couldn't let it go.

Maybe now he'd get some closure.

10
———

"**B**ungy jumping!" Izzie said with enthusiasm. Her eyes gleamed, and her skin shone as the golden light of the morning hit her cheeks. They had organised to meet at what was becoming their normal coffee spot, and Ethan tried not to gag on the mouthful of coffee he'd just chugged back.

His stomach did a loop the loop. "Bungy jumping," he repeated. Maybe he'd misheard her.

"Yeah. Doesn't it sound fun? Have you ever been before?"

No, and Hell no. "Nope. You?"

"Nah. I would never have been allowed! My bod—um—brother would never have let me. He's super protective like that."

Ethan squinted, his Ray-Bans protected Izzie from seeing his genuine expression. If he'd had to guess, he'd put money on the fact Izzie had nearly just said 'bodyguard'. Did that mean she was relaxing around him? It seemed so, but he still wasn't entirely certain what to believe about Isabella.

"Are you sure it's something you want to do?" He had to ask. Hope be damned.

"Double, triple sure. So you're in?"

Someone kill me. "Yeah, 'kay." He coughed a little, hoping to clear the wodge that was stuck in the back of his throat. A trickle of sweat appeared at the base of his back, even though it was barely three degrees and his fingers were frozen against a piping hot cup of coffee.

He followed her into the booking centre, noting she had an excited spring to her step whereas he walked as if going to prison.

One instructor met them inside, explaining the jump and having them sign some waiver paperwork. His grip on the pen threatened to snap it in two as he signed his life away. Still, he didn't miss Izzie's hesitation over her signature or how she scrutinised it for a second afterward, a little buckle appearing between her eyebrows.

There were a few others inside the office, most sporting the same excited expression as Izzie held with a few slightly anxious looks thrown in for good measure. His face gave away none of the dread he felt at this activity.

They loaded onto the bus, and to add to his torture—though this one being of a different nature—he had to squeeze in against Izzie, her thigh moulded to his. Every breath he took, he breathed in a cloud of her. She smelled divine, and it was almost enough to distract his thoughts from what was to come.

"You're quiet," Izzie said with a little sideways frown his way.

"Just enjoying the view."

That earned him a raised brow. "Of the highway?"

He shrugged. "Why do you want to do this?"

"Why don't you?" she quipped back.

"I never said I didn't want to do this." He leaned in, his shoulder bumping against hers as the bus went over a pothole. "And don't avoid my question."

"You didn't have to say it—your eyes are screaming with disdain."

Just as he didn't miss much about her, it would seem she wasn't missing much about him either. "I have a thing with heights."

"A thing? As in a fear? A loathing? A hatred?"

"D. All the above."

She let out a soft whistle. "What on earth are you doing coming along if you fear heights?"

Good question. He couldn't exactly tell her the truth, but then ... was that really the whole reason he was doing this? Part of him just didn't want to let her out of his sight. Increasingly he worried that had nothing to do with the job and everything to do with her being her. "Guess I thought it might help." His tone was dry, tinged with a little sarcasm.

Obviously she found it amusing as her lips split into a grin and she laughed right in his face. That laugh that told him she thought he was certifiably insane.

Maybe he was.

It was possible he would be after he dove off a bridge with nothing but a few buckles and a piece of stretchy rope to stop him plunging to his death.

Izzie struggled to focus on what the instructor was saying. Ethan was afraid of heights. Ethan Raines—who hadn't so much as flinched at anything else, who said he'd stepped in front of a sniper bullet that had killed someone—was afraid of heights.

Her own list of fears was long, but heights weren't on it. When she looked down into the ravine, she just saw rushing water and got a sense of excitement. She'd watched Ethan's face when he'd looked—it had taken on a grey tinge that had her worrying he would pass out.

She reached out, gripping his fingers. "You don't have to do this," she whispered.

He leaned towards her, his breath warm against her ear. "Bit late to back out now."

She shook her head at that, filled with admiration. He wasn't one to ever back down from anything. Even if it scared him witless.

As others jumped before them, her excitement shifted into nervousness. Her tummy did little flip-flops as each person jumped, letting out a scream as they fell straight down.

The speed of the jet boat had left her exhilarated. She wanted that rush again. She wanted to test the boundaries of her body and her mind. If she could do something as scary as bungee jumping, then surely she could confront her own worst fears. Those of her memories and of what her father thought of her. Of what she'd done.

"You ready?" Ethan asked her, a frown on his face. He searched her eyes, and she wondered if this was the first time he'd spoken to her or if he'd already asked a few times.

"Yep!" she replied with a false bravado. She nodded as the instructor repeated the information, giving her a smile of encouragement. She flicked her gaze to Ethan, who stood stoically behind her. It was seeing his face that made her feel good about this activity—it made her feel brave. Happy. Safe.

The cords were triple-checked, her harness pulled and prodded, ensuring all was as it should be. Her feet inched out onto the board that sat away from the bridge's edge. *Wowsers.* Standing here with nothing before her but a 43 metre drop left her knees feeling a little weak. The view was breathtaking, and she had a sense of freedom, a moment of clarifying silence. Had this been what her mother had been trying to find? That sense of being calm and at peace with oneself?

Her eyes fluttered shut, and she swallowed. She couldn't be sure she'd ever understand how her mother could choose to end her life. Depression wasn't something she'd experienced, and whilst she ached on the inside, she felt too much to ever want to end her life. From what she'd read, the depression had just taken away all of her mother's ability to feel until she was left with nothing but an urge to end it all. Could she forgive her mother for making that choice?

Maybe that was the step she had to take now. If she dived off this bridge, she'd do so with a promise to forgive her mother. Her breathing hitched.

"Izzie?"

Ethan spoke from somewhere behind her.

It was time to take her next step forward.

She jumped.

Ethan's heart leapt along with Izzie's body. It pitched forward, and he swore he could almost feel it in the back of his throat. Or maybe that was his breakfast. Bloody hell. She'd jumped. Actually jumped. *That means I'm next.*

Now his breakfast was definitely making a reappearance. Acid burned at the back of his throat and he cringed.

He shuffled to the right a little and peered over the edge. His head swam, and the world tilted, but he could see Izzie bobbing about on the end of the rope, arms outstretched, and through the rushing in his head he could hear her faint laugh. *She is fine.*

"All right, mate. You ready?"

Ethan turned to the dude who stood at the edge, only just registering the Aussie accent. "As I'll ever be," he replied with a stony voice.

The other guy laughed. "Your girl talk you into this, did she?"

He sucked in air. He wished Izzie were his girl, but unfortunately life was never that clear cut. He nodded at the other guy, figuring it would do. He was avoiding opening his mouth, in case it spoke his mind and called a stop to this insane idea.

They rolled the grips into place, clinking and flopping them against his leg. He looked down at the harnessing—it didn't seem enough, but then nothing ever would.

"All right. You're good to go, buddy. The things we do for the right girl, hey?" said Mr Aussie with a grin.

Ethan could only offer a lopsided grimace before he stepped off the ledge.

His eyes were welded shut, and he prayed on everything he could think of that he'd survive this fall with some part of his dignity intact. There was no excitement—his body was paralysed with fear. Air rushed past him and he waited for the inevitable impact. The rope would break. His head would smash through the water and he'd be drilled right into the bottom of the river. Time seemed to stretch, and he focused on one thought, one name.

Izzie.

There was a pulling sensation at his ankles as his speed slowed. Falling turned more to a feeling of floating and then he was tugged back up only to fall again. He swung a little, and he creeped one eye open, relief flooding through him as he realised it was over.

He turned to see Izzie over on the side, jumping and waving in excitement. Well, at least she'd enjoyed the show. *Never again.*

Once back on solid ground, he resisted the urge to pat down his body to check he was in fact still in one piece. He trudged over to the group only to be brought up short by the impact of Izzie's form leaping up and wrapping around him. He drank in her scent, gripping her close.

"I can't believe you did that," she whispered against his mouth.

His eyes caught hers and a different kind of paralysis took over. He was fighting a losing battle. Looking into her eyes now, shining bright with euphoria and something else … the slight change there. She appeared … happier. A little less lost. He searched those blue depths, knowing if he didn't pull away soon he was sunk.

She stole his chance, leaning in and brushing her lips against his.

Ethan struggled to keep his mind on the conversation. After everyone had done their jump, the bus drove them back into Queenstown and a few of them went to the pub to celebrate with a beer. Izzie had been in her element, chatty and bubbly, insisting they go too. Though he'd noticed she avoided being in any of the group photos, somehow always insisting she be the one to take them.

It had only been a quick kiss. You could barely even call it that.

Izzie was acting like it had been nothing but was avoiding his eyes a little.

"So you're an Aussie? Here for the snow, right?"

He turned to the guy beside him. Clean-shaven and of a slight build, he looked to be barely eighteen. Ethan took a sip of his beer, buying time and trying to remember if he'd been told this dude's name. Nate, maybe.

"Yep."

He didn't bother to ask anything in reply, not wanting to prolong any chat.

Izzie had kissed him. Had it been confusion that had crossed her face afterwards? The entire thing had been so brief he hadn't taken it all in properly before she'd jumped down and dragged him into the fold.

He didn't want to be here, pretending interest in a group of people who thought jumping off a bridge was fun.

He wanted to go somewhere and be alone with Izzie. He wanted to talk to her. He needed to ... *Jesus, what? What the hell can I say to her without breaking my promise to Ian?*

Sculling the last of his beer, he tried to catch Izzie's eye, but she was still studiously looking in a different direction.

He stood and walked around the group and crouched at her side, finally drawing her attention. "I've got a few calls to make. Can I catch you up in about an hour?"

"Sure," she replied, her focus on his shoulder.

He tilted his head, bringing his gaze into alignment with hers. "Sure?"

She gave him a tight smile and nod. *Dammit.* She was annoyed with him.

He left the bar, refusing to give in to the urge to look back at her. She was tying him up in knots and making him consider breaking rules. He should come clean—tell her that Ian had contacted him, that her family were worried.

Outstanding idea, Ethan, because she won't hate you at all if you admit you've been protecting her.

Hadn't she already outlined how she wanted space to think? How at home she had been crowded by her overprotective brothers. Admitting to her they had asked him to 'keep an eye on her' wouldn't end well for whatever this was between them.

He wasn't ready to define it, but he also wasn't ready for it to end.

His forward momentum stalled. Someone crashed into his back, sending him a dirty look as he muttered an apology. Should he go back? His feet decided for him—slow steps increasing with speed until he was jogging around the corner to the pub. Reaching for the door handle, it was wrenched away from him, pulled inwards to reveal Izzie.

"You came back," she blurted, her eyes wide with surprise. "Did you forget something?"

"Yeah. This." He stepped into her personal space and without waiting another beat, he kissed her, crushing her lips under his. He pulled her waist towards him, their bodies meeting from thighs to chest, his other hand taking over holding the door so it didn't knock them flying.

He stepped back, dragging her with him, all the while not breaking contact with her lips, which were giving as good as he was. How had he held off this long? She tasted divine. All hot summer sun and refreshing cold beer. Every muscle in his body seemed to relax. The tension in his shoulders he'd been holding onto for what seemed like forever drifted away.

She shifted away a little, her eyes fluttering open to drill into his. Hers were languid, heated and full of liquid fiery desire. He tightened at the sight. A slight groan escaped him when she bit her bottom lip then slid her tongue across the spot.

"I thought you had calls."

"This was more pressing."

She giggled. "Oh boy. You don't muck around when you go all in, do you?"

Unfortunately, every response that came to mind was superfluously corny and he just couldn't go there. Even if she was worth corny. Hell. She was worth everything. And knowing this was doomed didn't stop him lowering his head to those lips once more.

A car drove past—catcalls whistled in its wake. He needed to stop this. At least for now. Perhaps the walk back to his accommodation might knock some sense into his head. Or ice into his pants. He cringed at that thought. This was about so much more than that.

His lips nipped at hers before breaking away. "I think perhaps we need to go somewhere else more private. To talk," he added.

The corner of her mouth quirked in amusement. Her eyes were sparkling with heat and desire, and telling him without words that she very much wanted to be alone with him in private.

She bit her lip again, and he mentally doused himself in snow. *Give a man strength.* Grabbing his hand, she started walking, swinging their arms between them in leisurely happiness.

"I wasn't even sure you liked me," Izzie said after a while.

Ethan started at her words. "My spending practically every waking moment with you and ignoring the pristine powder snow daily didn't clue you in?"

She grinned at him. "Maybe you just felt sorry for me."

"Trust me, if that was all, I'd have bought you a hot chocolate and made my excuses."

"Guess I'll worry if you ever offer me a hot chocolate then."

His phone beeped from his back pocket and he fished it out, rolling his eyes when he saw it was his mum. He connected the call with a swipe of his thumb. "Mum."

"Hello, darling. I didn't expect to catch you. I figured you'd be up the slopes."

"Uh, no. Different plans for today."

"Another day of no skiing. I'm intrigued. Isabella must be quite a gal."

"Funny, Mum. Please tell me you haven't called to discuss my love life?"

"So it's love then?" She pounced.

Oh, man. Why the hell had he said that.

"Bye, Mum." He hung up.

A text beeped with a cute winking smiley face and a quick message saying she was happy for him. His chest warmed.

"Your mum is cute," Izzie said.

He stretched his neck, shrugging his shoulders to remove a bit of tension that had crept back in. "Yeah. She's nosy, but she means well."

Izzie squeezed his hand, and the stiffness in his shoulder relaxed a little. "She seemed surprised to catch you. Figured you'd be skiing?"

"The snow's not going anywhere."

"But I'm keeping you from it."

He cocked an eyebrow. He'd take the option of spending the day with her over skiing any day—hands down, no contest. But he wasn't ready to admit that. Yet.

"We could go tomorrow?"

"Yeah?" Ethan took in her nervous features and repeated her gesture, squeezing her hand. "Only if you're up for it. I'm keen, but I understand how memories can grip hold. If it's too soon ..."

"It's been over five years. I need to face these memories at some stage. Right?"

They turned the last corner that took them to their street. The hill slowed their progress to more of a meander. The sense of urgency that had gripped him at the pub simmered, delicious anticipation having taken hold. Ethan felt no need to rush this, wanting to enjoy every moment he had the pleasure of Izzie being his—without his job or her title getting in the way.

"Did you find out anything about your work?"

He jolted at her question before realising she meant the shooting and her theory about it being the wife. Not a direct correlation to his own thoughts. "Not yet. I spoke to the official investigator though, who promised to get back to me. It fits though, tying up some blank puzzle pieces we couldn't place. Maybe you need to reconsider your career path."

They were coming to the gate that led to the stone cottage she was renting. He hadn't yet been inside and left it for her to decide, pausing as they reached it.

"Maybe I do," she replied, an odd look on her face. "Can I meet you at yours in ten? I just want to take a quick shower after this morning's excitement."

Woah. If ever there was a time he needed to not have a visual of her naked in the shower ... He half choked but turned it into a cough. "Knock and come on in whenever you're ready." He glanced at his watch, it was after two. "Should I order a pizza or something? Lunch sort of got bypassed."

She leaned in and placed a kiss against his lips. "Sounds perfect."

He waited until the door closed behind her, pretending that he hadn't just ogled her pert behind the whole walk along the path.

Jogging across the road, he mentally organised how he'd fill that gap. He scrubbed at his jaw. Did he have time to shave? Ordering pizza had to come first. There was a bag of chips and dip in the cupboard. He could pull that out to keep them going. His heart beat an erratic staccato. Shower might have to wait. Maybe he could talk Izzie into joining him. That thought brought a quick grin to his lips.

After unlocking the door, he was barely two steps in when his phone rang. *Dammit.* He pulled it out and saw Cameron's name. As much as he wanted to ignore the call, he couldn't. "Raines."

"Ethan. I got bad news. Your hunch doesn't check out. She's squeaky clean."

Dammit times two. He'd been so sure. "We're missing something, Cameron. I just know we are."

"That might be the case, but I'm not sure we will find it with the wife."

"What about their personal finances?"

"What about 'em?"

"Did you look into them?"

"Mate, I can't just pull a person's financial records. I need a warrant and concrete evidence to get one. A hunch from an elite bodyguard will not hold up in court, my friend."

"Yeah, yeah," he said, holding in the urge to smash his hand against the counter.

"Later, buddy." The line dropped out.

The heat he'd been feeling surged into anger and frustration. He didn't know why he was so sure they were onto something. Izzie's throwaway comment had just clicked, and now he couldn't let it go.

He threw the phone onto the couch. Annoyed that it immediately beeped with an incoming message, he stooped to collect the offensive piece of metal. Ethan swiped with more vigour than the phone could handle, requiring another attempt until the message appeared across his screen.

Ethan, love. Just letting you know I'm on the way to the hospital. I've had a few pesky chest pains and thought I should let you know. If you get a minute, can you call me? Love, Mum.

Ethan's heart stuttered, and all but stopped.

11

Izzie had primped and preened in record time, putting on a clingy knitted dress she'd stumbled across in the window of a boutique on the main street. After slipping on her ankle boots with a studded butterfly pattern across the front, she ran her fingers through her hair in front of the mirror, tussling her locks into an effortless 'just rolled out of bed' look. She'd forgone make-up other than a quick swipe of lip gloss. Her skin was glowing with excitement. In fact, since being here, she'd felt lighter and healthier than she had in ages.

Not once had she drunk too much or hidden her pain behind an extra shot of vodka.

It had been a welcome reprieve.

The reflection that met her gaze had her standing taller. Nerves fluttered in her belly. Should she come clean? Would Ethan look at her differently?

She'd had a few slips of the tongue already, but not once had he said anything. He kept his thoughts so carefully guarded. A moment's hesitation was now turning into a second guessing game.

Stop! Ethan was a good guy. Somehow she'd known that the moment she'd met him, and his actions had only proved her hunch to be true.

He cared. He was a wonderful human. She could only hope he'd understand why she wasn't honest from the get-go. He was a bodyguard by profession, for crying out loud—if anyone understood the need for privacy and protection, well, it was him.

The only question was, did she tell him before they took things to another level? Or after?

Unable to make that decision, she turned on her heel, grabbed her bag and keys, and walked out, closing the door with a solid click behind her.

What if she told him and he rejected her? What if he walked away? Izzie was no fool. She'd had serious crushes on guys in the past, but not one of them had been privy to the real Isabella, with no smokescreen and no crown. She'd shown Ethan who she was. She'd invited him into her thoughts, her fears, and he'd returned the favour. Could she trust he'd understand that she was still the same person when he found out the truth?

The air was collecting a hint of cool. The day had started off shining and bright, but clouds had rolled in, obliterating the sunshine. It felt later than it was. Her stomach rumbled, issuing a mixed warning statement of hunger and antic- ipation.

She skipped up the front-deck steps, her boot heels clip- clopping against the wood. The view from the expansive deck was amazing, and she hoped to coerce Ethan out here later tonight when it would show nothing but a sea of lights sparkling before them.

After placing a gentle knock against the door frame, she slid the glass across, expecting to find Ethan waiting inside.

Instead she was met by a fast-talking and frustrated voice coming from the bedroom. His ski bag was packed and sat in the middle of the living room. Her mind skittered at that sight, her heart leaping into her throat as she picked out words from his conversation.

"Need to be on the next available flight …"

"Tomorrow … not okay."

"It has to be *today*."

He walked out of what she assumed was the bedroom, his face ashen. He flinched when he caught sight of her, a soft expletive could be heard from under his breath.

"I'll call you back," he said, then hung up. The phone lay limply in his hand before he started tapping it against his other hand. "This isn't what it looks like."

"So you're not desperately trying to get the next flight back to Sydney?"

"Okay. This is what it looks like then. My mum's in hospital."

Izzie stumbled to the side and slid into the armchair that was closest. "Is she … what happened?" She swallowed at the sudden dryness and ache in the back of her throat.

"Suspected heart attack. She messaged saying she was in hospital with chest pains. I called as soon as my phone beeped, but her phone was turned off. When I got through to the hospital, they said she'd had another episode. They were running tests. She was asleep. I need to go back to Australia." He ran a hand across his face, anguish lighting his features. "I'm sorry."

After pushing to her feet, she closed the gap in seconds, gripping him to her tight. "Don't be. Let me make a call." She pulled back to look him in the eye. "Do you trust me?"

He hesitated, a slight frown crinkling his forehead. "Yes."

"Give me a minute." She walked over to the bag she'd

dropped to the ground, collecting her phone, and then went to the deck to make a call.

Felix picked up after the second ring. "I'm in the middle of a dinner and about to make a speech."

"I need your help. I need to organise a private plane to fly us back to Sydney."

"Okay. Us?"

"Later, Felix. I don't have time to explain now. Ethan's mum is in hospital."

He sucked in a deep breath. He might not have a clue who Ethan was, but the word *mum* always hit a note with the Stenish siblings.

"I'll make a call. Stay by your phone." The line went dead.

Ethan came to stand beside her at the railing. He looked at her, his face still pale, a questioning expression in his eyes.

"My brother ... he has a lot of connections. He'll arrange a private plane for us."

"They must be some serious connections."

She shrugged, avoiding his gaze. Eventually if she wanted this to be anything serious, she'd have to tell Ethan everything. This wasn't the time, but she knew, deep in her gut, that she wanted serious. She wanted him. That would mean a whole new gamut of questions and logistics to consider. Her entire life was on the other side of the world. She might not be next in line like her oldest brother, but she couldn't move away from her home in Geravia.

Her mind wobbled. Ethan reached out and hooked a flyaway strand of hair behind her ear, and she flicked away all thoughts past today.

A beep on her phone had her racing it straight to her ear.

"A plane will be on the tarmac within the hour to fly you direct to Sydney. If you can get there to clear paperwork as soon as possible, that would help."

"Great. Thank you. I mean it."

"Yeah. It's booked under Isabella Correll." Her brother's words were a little stilted as he spoke her name. "Tell Ethan we're sending best wishes to his mum."

She nodded into the phone, her throat too tight to speak. The phone was taken from her hand, but Felix had already hung up.

"I was going to thank him," Ethan said.

"Another time. We need to move. Plane will be ready to go in an hour."

He turned to walk inside but then paused, his jaw locked. He flicked his eyes to hers. "You'll come?"

She'd planned to, invitation or no invitation, but it was nice to see the hopeful look in his green depths.

"Yes," she said simply. "I'll need twenty to pack up my stuff. I'll try to be fast."

He leaned in, grabbing her waist to pull her to him, crushing his mouth onto hers for a brief but intense kiss. It left her reeling, but she didn't have time to analyse. She had packing to do. Sydney, Australia and Ethan's mum were waiting.

Ethan tried not to let his worry show. Izzie had returned within fifteen minutes, bags packed and ready to leave. They'd driven to the airport in silence and were met by an airport official who organised Ethan's car return and took them through to a private lounge to wait whilst their passports were processed. He'd wondered if Izzie would have issues given she was European, but he guessed being a part of a royal family had its perks. Money talked. He might not know a lot about his father's birth country, but he knew it was a rich one.

Izzie sat beside him, legs crossed in an elegant pose, looking like a celebrity in the oversized armchair. She wore black sunglasses that covered half her face and had been tapping away on her phone for the duration since they'd sat.

"Something up?" he asked.

She flicked him a glance. "No. Just sorting out a few things." Her phone pinged again, but she tossed it into her bag without viewing the message.

Just who she was messaging?

"When we land, I've organised a car to take you straight to the hospital."

"Where are you going?"

She hesitated, then shrugged. "I'll find a hotel or somewhere to stay. Don't worry about me."

He swallowed, hoping to still some nervous energy that was coursing through his veins. "Do you want to come to the hospital with me?"

Her eyes widened a little. "I don't want to impose or be in the way."

"You wouldn't be. Actually, I'd like you to come. But only if you're okay with being there ..."

"I'd like that." A slight smile lifted her lips, and she reached out to grasp his hand.

They sat in silence until the flight attendant came to notify them that their plane was ready. Ethan's heart was still beating too fast, his pulse erratic as he tried not to think of the worst-case scenario.

Once they were seated, Izzie pulled her phone out again. She read a message quickly before switching off the device.

"Your mum is still asleep but stable. They should have the results for us when we arrive."

"Do I want to know how you found that out so quickly?"

She squirmed a little in her seat. "Can we just suspend those sorts of questions for a bit?"

He tried to block the hurt that her words brought on. Hell. He knew the answers to his own questions. But she didn't know that. It had become important to him for Izzie to *want* to tell him herself.

Nodding once, he gave her hand another squeeze before removing it again to double-check he was buckled tight. He'd flown in a private jet before—the luxury of this one not lost on him—but he didn't need details on how Izzie had secured this or whose it was. Hopefully Izzie would tell him everything in her own time.

He had to focus on being there for his mum. She was young still. Except for her preference for cake, she ate well and kept fit with a Pilates class once a week. She'd coerced him into going with him once. Never again. Was she stressed about something that she wasn't telling him?

He hadn't been the best son the past few years. In particular, the past six months. He'd allowed his work to consume him. Hadn't that been what his boss had said? That he was too invested—he needed to take a step back and find clarity. He needed to find balance.

When was the last time he'd gone to visit his mum just out of the blue? To hang out or take her for lunch? It wasn't like she lived far from his own unit in the city's outskirts. No. He'd just been so caught up in his work, he'd drifted into a void that included nothing else.

A fact he hadn't been able to see until this past week with Izzie. And now his mum had had a suspected heart attack. The thought clutched his own heart, squeezing until he gasped for air. The backs of his eyes felt hot, and he scrunched his hands into fists, fighting the lone tear that threatened to fall. He would not show weakness.

His mother would be fine.

From this point on he'd be there to make sure of it. It was time to make some changes in his life.

The hospital smelled like antiseptic. *Don't they all.* This one also had the omnipresent vibes of hope mixed with fear, terror and an underlying sense of urgency. Why were hospitals always so busy? People rushed everywhere. And why on earth did they always make them like a maze? As if they wanted you to forget any of your life-threatening illnesses and just get lost in a sea of corridors that offered cures. There were a lot of smiling faces in the cardiology ward.

Ethan's mother, Barbara, had been brought here after being admitted to emergency. By the time they'd arrived at the hospital, she was awake. And from the sounds of laughter and her ordering Ethan around inside the room, you'd never know she'd just suffered a heart scare.

Izzie hovered outside the private room, not wanting to interfere. She owed Henrik. Felix had texted saying it had been Henrik who'd called in a favour with a friend who was based in Queenstown and owned a private jet. Thank goodness he'd been at home and not off on business elsewhere. Her brother had also arranged for Barbara to have her own private room within the hospital. Izzie glimpsed flowers covering the side table—an abundant display of vibrant blooms interspersed with foliage that looked like floating green hearts. It was elegant, yet cheerful. Probably Eva or Sophia's doing, that one.

She stopped pacing and leaned against the hospital walls, staring up at the fluorescent lights. She didn't hate hospitals, but they weren't her favourite place in the world. They'd taken her mother to the hospital in Geravia—hours too late.

Hours.

That was another of the things her father had shouted at her. '*How dare you allow your mother to lie there for hours?*' A question she still couldn't ask herself without the familiar onset of panic. She hiccupped back the feelings.

No. Hospitals weren't her favourite. And like everyone else who disliked them, she had excellent reason.

It was funny to have such a strong association with a place when she'd only ever entered one a handful of times. The time Felix had broken his arm doing a backflip off the wall at the palace. The time she'd had to have her tonsils out. Both had occurred at a young age. Neither had been bad. She wouldn't call the visits pleasant, but they hadn't left a black mark on her heart.

She had gone to the hospital the day after her mother ... She'd forced herself to go. And she'd hated herself ever since. Her mother had looked like an ice queen, like sleeping beauty. Except no kiss from a handsome prince could ever bring her back.

"Hey, Izzie?"

She startled, swiping a hand at the tears that silently drizzled over her cheeks.

"Are you okay?" Ethan's voice instantly turned to concern, and he crouched by her side. "Has something happened?"

"No. Sorry, it's nothing." Throwing any elegance out the window, she did a full face swab against her shoulder. "Just tired and emotional. Girl stuff."

He sent her an arch look that said he didn't believe her, but thankfully let it slide. He traced a finger down her cheek, and it came away glistening with a single tear. Leaning in, he placed a lingering kiss against her lips. It sent a full body sigh through her, like a blanket being thrown around her shoulders to ward off all the cold and unwanted feelings.

"Mum was hoping to thank you. She couldn't believe how quickly we got here, and how nice the room is. Apparently peonies and maidenhair fern are her favourites." He shook his head and muttered, "Whatever they are."

"Flowers and greenery."

"Yeah, okay, smarty-pants. So you up for meeting my mum?" The look on his face was relaxed, giving off a whatever attitude, but his eyes spoke volumes. His mum was his entire family, and she was important to him. Which meant meeting her was important.

Her palms itched, and she wished she could have at least taken a moment to make herself look more presentable. What if Barbara didn't like her?

Oh, stop being ridiculous.

For once, she listened to her inner self without a second thought.

"I'd love to."

She accepted the hand he held out and was enveloped in another cosy warmth as his arm slid around her waist, marking her as someone important to him.

His mum was exactly as Izzie had pictured her from their brief chat on the phone. She was on the short side, with middle age showing beautifully in her warm and inviting embrace. Her personality fizzled around her, bright and welcoming, with hair an unnatural shade of mahogany, bordering on burgundy. It was cut short and highlighted the bottle-green eyes so similar to Ethan's. Just like his, they also didn't seem to miss a trick, instantly zeroing in on her son's hand clutching tight at Izzie's waist. Her lips twitched with a little amused satisfaction.

"So, you're Izzie? I have so much to thank you for. I'm not sure where to start. And gorgeous to boot! Speaking of, you must tell me where you got those boots—I want some."

Izzie couldn't help but laugh. It was no wonder Ethan didn't mind the daily check-in calls from this woman. She was the type of mum everyone wanted to have as their own. The affection between the two was obvious, and Izzie relaxed within their presence.

Barbara regaled them with a few tales of gossip from her local Pilates class. Apparently the instructor had run off with one of her students—a problem because she was married to the other instructor. The husband had exacted revenge by changing the wife's classes to different varieties of Pilates. Wine Pilates and bring-your-dog Pilates had been Barbara's favourites. Ethan was laughing, and Izzie could tell a weight had lifted from him.

They didn't stay long, the nurses ordering them out so Barbara could rest. Ethan promised they'd visit again first thing in the morning and it pleased Izzie he'd so easily included her without consultation. Everything with him just felt so right. So easy. So ... perfect.

How the hell was she going to break the news to him that this wasn't her normal life?

12

The taxi sped through the city which was still bustling even though it was late at night. The lights out the window dazzled, and she had to concede that Sydney at night was a sight to behold. Not as beautiful as Geravia, but then she was biased.

A small pang twisted in her heart. She was missing home.

Unfortunately, she still had no answers to her problem. Whilst she hadn't felt the same overwhelming panic at random situations or woken in a sweat every morning, it was all still there, waiting to creep up on her. No. She hadn't faced her demons yet. But at least she'd acknowledged they were there.

That was progress, right?

Something told her that Ethan could help her. If only she'd let him. She needed to let him in properly. Not this half effort she was making. He knew nothing of her genuine life lived in the public eye and filled with pressure, scheduled down to the minute.

She was lucky to have escaped this long without being

harassed by media. This far more relaxed and normal pace of life was really growing on her.

After about half an hour, Izzie realised she'd drifted off when the taxi pulled up in front of a neat-looking town house. Ethan leaned forward, paying the driver with cash before he grabbed their bags and led her to the front door. It was a pale lemon, very calming, with a cute, manicured front garden.

"You garden?"

"No. I'm the person who can kill a cactus. There's a gardener who looks after all of that as part of the strata." He pushed in the door and held it open as she walked through.

A nervous energy took over as Izzie stepped across the threshold. "Ha. I can relate on the gardening front. I wouldn't know the first thing to do. My mum was amazing. A real green thumb. She loved nothing more than to spend hours in her garden. In fact, my dad organised for her to design this amazing rose maze with some acclaimed horti-culturist. It's beyond beautiful and has been featured in tonnes of magazines. There's a team of gardeners who keep it in pristine condition. Not that it sees many visitors. My mum wanted it to be open for people when they came to the palace, but after she died, my dad closed it off. Gosh, I'd love even a tenth of her talent. Gardening seems very relaxing." She was totally rambling. *Time to stop talking, Izzie.*

"Palace?"

Izzie froze at Ethan's question. *Oh no. I said palace.* Her mouth opened and closed, probably making her look like a guppy, before she let out a laugh that sounded fake. "Uh, yeah. Our house is enormous. Family joke. We call it the palace. It's probably not really funny, is it?" *Terrible liar.*

He shrugged, but a funny look crossed his face. If

pushed, she'd have said it was disappointment. But that made little sense. Why would he be disappointed?

"I'll show you to the guest room. If you're feeling anything like me, I reckon I could sleep for a week. Today's news shaved ten years off my life."

She reached out and rubbed his arm. It was meant as a comforting gesture, but the minute she touched his skin, her body ignited from within. "She'll be fine." Her voice wavered.

Ethan stepped closer. He lingered, searching her eyes before he dipped his head and kissed her.

It was soft, almost hesitant, asking for permission. She tilted her head, shifting so she could kiss him back with more enthusiasm. She sighed, little shivers of delight dancing down her spine with every touch of his lips to hers.

The kiss changed, becoming more playful with tiny nips. His mouth skittered across to kiss the side of her mouth, then dragged across her jawbone and to the pulse at the base of her neck. Her head dipped, giving him better access.

"You should come with a warning," she murmured.

His hand slid to cup the back of her head, bringing it into alignment with his own. "Is that a complaint?"

"Oh no. Far from it, in fact."

Kissing Ethan Raines was one of Izzie's new favourite activities. She pushed at his jacket, helping him shrug it off. It landed on the ground behind them with a *thunk*. Her fingers tiptoed to the edge of his shirt, feeling the grainy cotton between her fingers. Her nails brushed smooth, warm skin, and he hissed.

"Woman, you are enough to slay an army." He chuckled against her lips.

"I don't want an army. Just you."

"Just me, hey?" He cocked a brow at her.

She flung her arms out wide and locked them about his neck, cocking her head to the side. "Yep. You and only you." She grinned. "Still tired?" Her grin turned cheeky.

His head dipped, and he glanced to the ceiling before bringing it back to look at her. The mood shifted with her question. His hands ran from her hips along the side of her body and lower, creating goosebumps over every inch they covered.

"Not so much." He sighed, but with a heavy overtone, giving Izzie a clue to the fact they weren't precisely on the same page. "But I also think we need to pause and decide if we're ready to take this next step."

"Oh," Izzie exclaimed, surprised by his words. She followed with a physical step back, her arms dropping from his shoulders to flop limply at her sides. "I guess I thought ... never mind. You're right. This is too soon." Inexplicable hurt assaulted every part of her body, narrowing in on her chest.

She went to bypass Ethan and make for the stairs behind him, but he grabbed her hand, stilling her movements. "Don't run away. I'm not turning you down. I want to be with you, Izzie. So much it aches. Especially in here." He patted his heart with his spare hand. "But I think you have demons you're fighting inside, truths you're not facing. And I think until you have, what we have needs to stabilise where it is. You're too important to me for us to rush this."

His words hurt, but only because they were dead on the truth. "I wasn't running," she muttered, sounding petulant. God, he was so right. She was still a mess. Hadn't she thought the same thing herself earlier?

"I'm falling for you." His words were quiet, but she heard every one as if he'd shouted it right in her face with a megaphone.

Her eyes flew to his—a truth there that she wanted to clutch hold of.

"Say something." He gave her hand a brief shake.

"I ... you're right. There are things I'm trying to sort out." Her eyes shifted downwards, focusing on the polished wooden floors. "Information about me I haven't shared with you, that I need too. I'm just not sure how you'll respond, and well ... you're important to me ... too." Her mouth was arid dry, and she desperately wished for a glass of water.

Cool fingertips touched her chin gently, tilting her gaze to his. "I'm not going anywhere, Isabella. The moment you're ready to talk, I'll be here. Always."

Was it possible to drown in someone's eyes? It certainly felt like it at the moment. Dragging her chin off his fingers, she darted around him and up the stairs. She needed space. This was too much. Her heartbeat was rapidly reaching supersonic speeds and her head was spinning. Was she about the have another panic attack? This was different though. This felt ... more real. As if it was coming from within her soul—not her mind trying to protect her from memories she didn't want to face.

"Izzie?"

Reaching the top of the stairs, she paused. "Yes?"

"Third door on the left. Clean towels are in the bathroom. I'll bring your bag up in a minute and leave it outside your door." His voice sounded a little broken. Conflicted, maybe.

At least that explained his disappointment from earlier. He'd guessed she was hiding something from him ... and had been hoping she'd open up. But did she really want to?

Offering a quick nod, she walked down the corridor, enjoying the feel of her socked feet falling into the plush carpet. She gripped the door handle and pushed inwards. After locating the light switch, she plunged the room into brightness. The door clicked shut behind her and an overwhelming wave of exhaustion flooded her. Five steps to the bed and Izzie crashed face first into the soft, white cotton, burying her view of the world.

Ethan was falling for her and she him. She couldn't deny those feelings were increasing daily. He got her—was showing a level of patience and understanding she hadn't experienced with anyone in a long time. But would that change when he found out she was a princess? Would he still believe she was the same person?

And what of her reasons for being here? She'd travelled halfway around the world, had run away from her home to find a solution to the issues that had slowly been taking over her life since her mother died. She'd tried to rediscover Princess Isabella—the confident, happy, bubbly girl who had big dreams.

Sure, she'd been putting on an excellent show for everyone for years, but deep down that wasn't how she'd been feeling, was it? Deep down she'd always had this crushing sense that she'd let her mother and father down. It was *that* that she needed to resolve. But how did one fix an issue like the one she had with her father? Would he ever even look her in the eyes again without blaming her?

She might have tried to forgive herself for not going to someone sooner that night, but she couldn't say she had succeeded on that score either. If she couldn't forgive herself, how on earth could he?

Izzie had been out for hours, her mind befuddled with too much alcohol. She'd gone to find her mum, wanting a hug. The boyfriend had been a douche. Not interested in her for her, only her title. Hadn't her mum warned her of something similar before she'd gone out that night—that exact fact had caused their argument.

Her mum hadn't been in her room, nor the library where she could often be found. Izzie had wandered out into the early morning, deciding to check the maze. Her mum sometimes walked there first thing.

The slow meander through various blossoming roses had been delightful, if not a little wobbly. But it was the sight at the end that had stilled her heart and forever changed her life.

Her mother, lying cold on the wooden-slatted bench chair. Her skin whiter than the snowy roses that surrounded her. The canopy of wisteria moody and sinister in the partial light.

A scream had risen inside her, desperate to escape, but it hadn't. It was as if her body had shut down, incapable of functioning at any level.

Was she dreaming? Run. It was time to run from the image she never wanted to see.

When would she stop running?

Ethan delivered Izzie's bag to her door, leaning in to see if he could detect any movement. He heard soft, even breaths, indicating she'd already fallen asleep.

His body ached, parts of it accusing him of his mind impeding its physical satisfaction. As much as he wanted to be with Izzie, he'd made the right decision. If nothing else, there was an entire world of dishonesty between them. How was that a suitable way to start a relationship?

Why the hell had he made that promise to Ian about not telling Izzie anything? It was eating at him—the lie. Not that it was anything terrible. He hadn't officially signed a contract. He wasn't accepting money to monitor her ... but that was splitting hairs. He was still being dishonest. He knew that was how she'd see it.

Trust wasn't something that came easily to those in positions such as hers. He'd witnessed how well she kept up a show of happiness whilst holding people at bay. But he'd seen underneath that. She'd invited him in to glimpse the real Isabella, and what he saw made him ache with want. Whatever she was running from, he wished more than anything she'd just share it with him. How could he help or fight any battles for her if she wouldn't tell him?

After padding back down the stairs with silent footsteps, he walked into the kitchen and pulled a beer out of the fridge. He flicked the top off using the bench and took a deep drag of the bitter liquid. It swirled down his throat, satisfying one hunger—if not the others he was feeling.

On a whim, he pulled his phone out, and not bothering to check the time difference, he hit dial on Ian's number. It rang for a few beats before it connected.

"Hart."

"We're back in Sydney. I thought you should know."

"How is Barbara?"

Ethan narrowed his eyes at the question, choosing to ignore it and focus on the other implication. "If you have someone else watching us, you don't need me anymore."

"No. I don't have anyone else watching. Prince Henrik informed me of the changes. I still need you in your current position."

Ethan swore under his breath. "Must I still do this? You know where she is. You know she's safe."

"Why don't you want the job anymore?"

"It's not a job. It's a favour ... Don't call it something it isn't."

"I see." The other man's inflection changed a minuscule

amount, but it was enough for Ethan to swear again. This time silently.

"No. It's not like that."

"Then how is it?"

"We're friends. I'm lying to her."

"You're protecting her. There's a difference."

Ethan placed his beer on the counter with considerable patience given he felt like exploding with the frustration that was coursing through him.

Before he could speak, Ian continued, "Ethan, if word gets out that Izzie is gallivanting about with no protection, the media will have a field day. Never mind who else. Stenaco might be at peace right now, but it's no secret the country is prosperous, and the royal family are well off. They have their fair share of enemies. She's at risk of being kidnapped, ransomed—I need not paint more of that picture to you, need I?"

"Then bring her home. You know where she is."

"And *you know* why that's a terrible idea."

"Then have her father call her—have him apologise and call her home."

"She hasn't told you everything then."

"Dammit, Ian, no she hasn't! This is like putting a puzzle together only to realise half the pieces aren't even in the box. I'm ..." ... *compromised.* Was he really going to admit that? After all he'd done to fight for his job and his position, was he just going to give in to this pattern of screwing up?

No. He couldn't do it. He was developing feelings for Izzie, but admitting that to Ian was tantamount to admitting he'd screwed up. All over again.

"You're?" Ian asked.

"Never mind. Mum's fine." He hung up.

Man, his dad would have ripped him a new one if he'd known what was going on. The job came first. Always.

For now, he'd just have to continue as things were, and hope that Izzie decided to go home on her own. His mum should be discharged from hospital tomorrow or the day after. If he brought her here to stay, he'd have an added barrier to what he was feeling for Izzie. Plus, if anyone could get her to talk, it was his mum. She couldn't be anywhere without people spilling their guts to her—a trait she thankfully hadn't passed on.

He had a plan. Now to implement it and get his head together.

Starting with the ground rules of no more kissing his runaway princess.

13

─────

"It's such a beautiful day out today. How about Izzie and I go hang at my house? I need to attend to my geraniums before they stop talking to me and die out of spite."

Izzie raised her brows at Barbara, amused by her not-so-subtle suggestion that they escape Ethan for the day.

They'd all been staying in his town house for the past three days since the hospital had discharged Barbara with strict diet and exercise rules. No overdoing it, essentially, which had been fine for the first day when Barbara had capitulated to Ethan's demands and taken it easy. Now she was champing at the bit to have her own freedom. Izzie should know. She'd become the person in the middle who both had whined to about the other. It was hilarious. Not having lived in such proximity to others and amid such close family dynamics, with the bonus of unquestioning love, she was enjoying the change. It gave her a new feeling of belonging and safety that had been missing.

"Okay," Ethan said, nodding over the cup of coffee he gripped in his right hand. He'd been out for a run, his long-sleeved, figure-hugging shirt showcasing a tantalising view, complete with a sweat patch running south from the V. "Let me shower and I'll come with you."

"You're not invited, darling. I love you, but three days living with you reminds me too much of your teenage years."

He raised a brow. "I see."

"Don't get in a snit. I promise I'll deliver us both back later this afternoon, safe and sound. We could pop into that lovely deli around the corner from my house and pick up ingredients for dinner. They have the most delicious pastas and fresh produce." The latter she spoke directly to Izzie.

Izzie chose not to comment, lest she end up in the middle of an argument. Instead she just offered an encouraging nod.

"How do you plan to get there?"

"Well, I can take your car, sweetheart. Or if that will annoy you, how about you drop us there, then I can bring us back in my car. In fact, that's probably better. Then I'll have it here. Surely we're reaching the point where I can go back to living in my own home soon. I know you mean well, but you can't be thinking I'll stay here indefinitely."

Izzie hid a laugh at the comical look on Barbara's face— one that was a mix of patronising, love and mothering. The look only a mother can pull off. It was especially funny considering Ethan was a giant compared to his mum who was petite.

"I presume anything I say will be ignored. I'll grab a shower and be ready to take you whenever." He pushed his chair back from the table and left the room.

"Thank you, honey," Barbara called after his retreating back.

The other woman beamed and Izzie felt sorry for Ethan.

But only a tiny bit. She was excited to have the day alone with his mum. Since the night of the non-progressive kiss and Ethan's statement, he'd gone to an additional level of stand-offishness. It was killing her. Not that having any intimate time with his mum around was feasible, but it wasn't even that. It was his attitude towards her. He'd barricaded himself behind a friend-zone banner. It was so frustrating.

Gone were the subtle brief touches and looks that left her heart ping-ponging like table tennis. It was more like she'd become a job to him.

Job. That was something she hadn't thought about in a few days. Felix hadn't been bugging her either. He'd sent one text in response to her thank-you message—a message she'd sent to both brothers. Henrik hadn't responded. Eva had sent her a picture message yesterday containing a sketch that had been amazing, but Izzie had spent little time looking at it, as it was a reminder of her promise. The ball was still a few weeks away, but it signalled a permanent end date to her time here. Which meant a permanent end date with Ethan.

"How are you in the garden?"

Izzie opened her mouth but not much came out other than a garbled non-response which left Barbara laughing.

"We can work with that. How are you at baking?"

"Baking skills probably about the same. I'm not really all that good at much."

"Oh, sweets. That's rubbish. You're good at lots of things."

"How do you know? You barely know me."

"Well, you've made my son beam and laugh like I've not seen him do since his father died, so that makes you qualified for anything in my books." She stood and walked over to Izzie, leaning down and giving her a warm hug.

Something inside Izzie cracked, and she slammed her eyes shut, enjoying the moment. "Thank you," she said, hoping the hitch in her voice didn't show.

"I'll go get ready too. We can leave whenever you're good."

Izzie sucked in a few deep breaths. There was a deep bond between Ethan and his mother, which was both beautiful and heart-wrenching for Izzie to witness. But Barbara's embrace had felt like a mother's hug.

She waited for the panic to take hold as she let memories of her mother into her mind. How she'd always smelled of roses. How she'd loved royal blue—the colour that had brought her eyes to life the most. Eyes that were so similar in colour to Izzie's.

Izzie stood. Taking her breakfast dishes into the kitchen, she loaded them into the dishwasher as she'd seen the others do. She felt an odd sense of satisfaction when she'd finished. After taking the stairs two at a time, she marched into the bedroom she'd claimed as her own. Her clothes were strewn about the place, the bed in total disarray. Her mother had always joked she slept like a drunk octopus. It was a fact she couldn't refute.

Time to start spring-cleaning her life. She hadn't been able to do much about her insides, but she could start in another location. Leading a tidier more normal life seemed to make sense. Hadn't her mother always joked that even though she'd become a princess, and then a queen, not once had she ever forgotten where she'd come from or what values she'd been raised with.

Izzie used to be a tidier person. When had she let those values go to the wayside?

Don't answer that.

Enough self-recriminations. She walked over to the bed

and flinging the quilt back, she searched for her sheet, finding it in a rolled and discarded mess towards the end of the bed. After pulling it up, she fluffed the doona over the top before smoothing the edges and placing the pillows in place. There. That looked better.

Next she collected the strewn pieces of clothing and folded them into a neat pile in her suitcase. There was a built in within the room, but she hadn't been able to bring herself to use it. She worried if she went that far, she may never leave.

Changing into some leggings and a slouchy, comfortable knit dress, she then added white converse sneakers and unearthed her canvas hat. She walked over to the mirror and checked out her reflection. The blonde who stared back at her looked funky, stylish, but more than anything, she had a tinge of pink in her cheeks that spoke of happiness. Her eyes were bright. Wow. She looked just like her mum. *I don't think I've ever noticed how much I look like mum ...*

The thought left an unpleasant taste in her mouth—like she'd missed something that was of utmost importance.

Turning away, she grabbed her cross-body bag and walked out of the room. Normally she'd close the door behind her, but today she left it open. There were things in her bag that were a dead giveaway of who she really was. Her genuine passport for one. But leaving the door open felt like a step towards telling Ethan the truth.

Bring on a fun day with his mum. Maybe she could find out what Ethan's favourite food was ... Barbara could surely help her make it. Then when the time was right, she could cook it for him and tell him everything, tearing down whatever barriers stood between them. It was becoming increasingly clear to Izzie that walking away from Ethan wasn't an option anymore. Which meant she needed to find a way to have him in her life.

Permanently.

Dappled sunlight scattered over Izzie's knees. Barbara's garden wasn't a tiny little side space like Ethan's—it was an expansive area behind her two-storey house. The house itself was beautiful. It wasn't new or full of the latest fashions, but it felt welcoming. It had been an interesting feeling to experience when she walked through the front door.

Ethan hadn't come in, choosing to just drop them off and stating he had a bit of work to attend too. Izzie had chosen not to say anything, knowing that he was still on forced leave. He'd confided to her that his boss had extended it after hearing about his mother's heart scare.

He'd taken the news in his stride, leaving Izzie to wonder what exactly he was off to do today. Probably just making himself scarce, given that was what his mum had requested. Would he enjoy the solitude after having so many people around in his space?

It was a thought that brought home exactly how little time they'd known each other.

She'd figured it might shake her earlier decision, but it didn't. Funnily enough, it just gave her more to look forward to finding out about him.

"You planning to squat there and daydream all day? Those weeds won't be plucking themselves," Barbara said with a meaningful voice.

Busted. "I'm just going to reiterate that gardening isn't my strong suit. So if I pull out anything that's not a weed, I apologise."

"You'll be fine. I feel it's in your blood."

"Why? I mean, what gives you that feeling?"

"No idea. I was hoping it would inspire you."

Izzie laughed, then did as she was told and dived in. She pulled and dug and settled into the task set to her. It wasn't until the sun hit her shoulders in a way that burned that Izzie realised she'd completely lost herself in her task. She'd cleared a patch that probably equated to a square metre—so not a lot of progress—but it had been relaxing. More so than she'd thought.

"See, it's in your blood."

Izzie stared at the cleared brown dirt before her. Sitting at its centre was a healthy-looking, leafy plant that featured a lone flower unfurling from its middle. "My mum loved to garden."

"Did you ever garden together?"

She shifted, sitting with her legs crossed instead of kneeling. Her legs tingled with the change in blood flow. "I used to help, if you could call it that. Mainly I sat or lay on the ground nearby just chatting." She smiled, but it held a tinge of sadness. "Moaning about boys," she scoffed.

"I'd have loved a daughter. I think it might have evened out Ethan's views a little."

Izzie looked over at the other lady, noting the melancholy expression that had come over her face. "What do you mean?"

"I lost my William to his job. He took a bullet to the heart. Ethan was eight. Goodness, how he'd idolised his dad. The two were inseparable whenever William was at home, which wasn't as often as I'd have liked. We were there the day he was shot. We'd moved overseas, back to William's home country after he'd taken a job there. We loved living there, but after he died, it was just too painful to stay. I wanted to be back here, so I had family close by. I worry the move here erased all memories for Ethan of his father. I think if Ethan had had a sibling, he wouldn't have taken the death so hard. It was like he grew up overnight, deciding he only had one path."

"He takes his job seriously."

"Sure does. Too seriously. Actually, this is the longest break I've ever had him on. It's nice to see him smiling and relaxed." Barbara threw her a pointed, mischievous look.

Izzie shook her head a little but smiled. "I like your son —a lot. But I'm afraid there are things standing in the way of us."

"Like countries and one giant, fat ocean? Ethan told me you're from Stenaco."

Izzie frowned. "Yes. Ethan mentioned that's where you'd been living ..."

"Serendipity."

She drew a little pattern on the side of her leggings. *Serendipity. Was it that?*

"All right. I think we've been melancholy enough now. Time for a late morning tea. How do you take your coffee?"

"Oh no! Let me go organise it. You're not meant to be overdoing it."

"Nonsense. Putting bickies on a plate and making cuppas isn't taxing. Besides, you look like you've got more thinking to do." Barbara groaned theatrically as she stood, leaving Izzie sitting on the grass in solitude.

"Thank you," she called out belatedly.

It was understandable that Barbara would have been itching to get back home. It was a beautiful spot, and the backyard was spacious and relaxing. She lay back on the grass, enjoying the sunshine on her face. The air was still cool, so the heat was welcome. Using her hand to block the glare, she let her mind drift, watching the clouds and picking out shapes.

Time stretched out. It was odd that out of all the people she could have had a luggage mix-up with, it had been Ethan, who had his own link to her country. Was that the world telling her something? That no matter how far she ran, she'd never be rid of her roots?

Not that she wanted to be. Increasingly, she was feeling pangs of homesickness. It didn't last long, but it was occurring most days now.

Would Ethan be interested in a trip to Geravia with her? Perhaps she could ask once she'd found the courage to come clean.

How long does it take to make coffee?

Deciding she'd help, Izzie stood, brushing off the grass from her legs. She stifled a yawn with her hand. The relaxed pace would be hard to give up when she returned home.

The screen door squeaked a little as she slid it across. It was strangely quiet in the sunroom. Continuing through to the kitchen, she looked around, but it was empty. A packet of biscuits was open on the counter. A plate sat beside it, along with two mugs next to the kettle. Izzie stepped forward, peering into the cups to see they contained coffee granules. She flicked the switch to boil the water again.

"Barbara? Do you take milk?" she called out, but was met with only silence.

A tinge of fear crept into her stomach.

It's probably nothing. Maybe she had to go to the bathroom?

Poking her head into the lounge room, she was yet again met by silence. She called out again. Nothing. The tinge grew, and her heart rate spiked. Turning on her heel, she jogged back through the kitchen, out another door and up the corridor to check the bathroom. Also empty.

She heard a soft moan.

"Barbara!"

There it was again. It was coming from one bedroom. Izzie raced into the first one and stalled just inside the entrance. Barbara was on the floor, eyes closed, her face a deathly shade of white. The image sent her flying into a whirl of fear, her mind shutting down. Not again. She couldn't go through this again.

The small sound of her voice tried to poke through Izzie's consciousness. *You need to move, Izzie. If you don't help her, she could die.*

She squeezed her eyes shut, seeing her father leaning over the dining room table. The floor beside the table was coated with shattered crystal and blood-red wine. His face was red—veins in his forehead all but bursting as he screamed at her. Screamed that she'd failed. If only she'd told someone when she'd first found her ... Margot would still be alive. The image changed, and this time it was Ethan. He was looking at her, accusation rife across his features, pure hatred shining in those green eyes.

Snap out of it, Izzie. You have to do something.

Ethan's eyes pierced the frozen state of her body and she went into overdrive.

Izzie checked Barbara's wrist for a pulse. It was there— faint, but there. "Barbara?"

She moaned again in response.

Izzie's breath whooshed out, her lungs almost collapsing from having held onto the stale air for too long. She fumbled in her back pocket before pulling out her phone with hands that shook.

Crap. What number do you call for emergency? Google gave her the answer, and she dialled and relayed whatever information she could with a voice that sounded far away, and far from hers. She was told to stay on the line—they'd track her phone. A tear slid down her cheek, plopping onto her knee.

"Hang in there, Barbara. Help is on the way," she whispered. *God, please don't be too late.*

She couldn't live with herself if she failed someone else.

14

For the second time within the space of a week, Ethan rushed into Sydney's Royal Prince Alfred Hospital. He'd broken the speed limit getting here and may have earned himself a ticket at one of the traffic lights, but he didn't care. The moment he'd heard Izzie's voice on the line—her tone as she'd tried to piece together a sentence—he'd known something was wrong.

He saw her before she noticed he'd arrived. She was sitting on the couch in the waiting room outside emergency, her knees tucked against her chest, arms loosely linked around her ankles. Her face was very pale, and he as he walked closer, he could make out silent tears rolling down her cheeks.

"Izzie?"

She jumped up, taking two strides towards him and throwing her arms around his neck. "The doctor's in with her now. They think she had a heart attack. A proper one this time. They mentioned operation. I, uh, should warn you I told them we were married."

He leaned back to see her face, which looked a little sheepish. "Okay …"

"They wouldn't tell me anything unless I was family."

He smiled. "Good thinking. Thank you for your quick action and calling the ambulance. That's twice now you've come to mine and my mum's rescue. Perhaps I *should* marry you." The words were out before he'd considered them properly. Izzie's eyes went wide, but before she could reply, a tall man with glasses came towards them.

"Ethan Raines?" he asked, his gaze flicking between the two.

"Yes." Ethan stepped forward, his hand outstretched, which the other man took.

"I'm Doctor Emmett Shaw. Your mother has suffered a myocardial infarction, but is now stable. Her ECG is showing minimal damage, but we need to get her started on new medication to get this under control. Two vessels are blocked. Did she tell you she hadn't been taking the medication as directed after her episode earlier this week?"

"What! No. She said she was. Dammit, Mum." Ethan scrunched his fingers into fists. A soothing hand found his back, but he couldn't look at Izzie. Anger and frustration coursed through him. Didn't his mum understand how important this was? How critical?

"Does she smoke?"

"No."

"Okay. She said no, but always good to check with another family member. She's had high blood pressure readings according to her doctor who advised a diet plan which she refused. Perhaps she'll listen now." The doctor offered a lopsided smile. "She'll be fine if she just makes a few life changes."

"Thank you." Ethan shook the doctor's hand again.

"The nurses will be out in a bit to take you in to see her." He nodded at Izzie before leaving them alone again.

"What was she doing?" His voice was hard and Izzie flinched, her hand dropping from where she'd been rubbing his back. He swallowed, aiming to tone it down a notch. "Sorry, I'm not meaning to sound like I'm blaming you. I don't at all."

"We were outside, doing some weeding. It wasn't strenuous, I promise. I was keeping an eye on her. She went to go make morning tea. When she hadn't returned, I went in to offer help and ..." Izzie hiccupped, her face draining of all colour. "I ... found her in the bedroom."

"Are you okay?"

She shook her head, fresh tears streaming down the tracks that were already drying on her face. "What If I'd been too late?" She choked out, her breathing laboured.

He placed his hands on either side of her face, turning her to focus on him and only him. Capturing her gaze in his, he searched, finding pain—raw and brutal—leaving him wondering if this was about more than his mother. "I need to see Mum, but afterwards, can we talk?"

She nodded, understanding flashing across her face. He led her back over to the seats, cocooning her in his arms as she burrowed in at his side. Her body felt fragile and extra small. It shook, her muffled sobs breaking something inside him, and he pulled her in tighter.

After a while, she calmed, one hand reaching out to clasp his other hand across his lap. They sat there waiting. Nurses bustled about, but whenever he caught one of their eyes, they just shook their heads. After the third such encounter, he let out a sigh, his head dipping back to hit the concrete wall behind him.

"What did you get up to today?" Izzie asked out of the blue.

Was she attempting conversation as a distraction? "Not a lot. I went to see Cameron, the investigator, but no news on the case. I called my boss, who told me I wasn't cleared to return yet. Apparently both Mum and I are on house arrest."

"She'll be okay. You'll make sure of it."

"The cakes will definitely go. Mum loves to bake. It will break her heart to follow some rigid diet to bring her cholesterol and blood pressure down."

"Maybe. Or maybe she can just find fresh ideas—new things to bake that just have less of the nasty stuff in them." Izzie shifted, pushing into a seated position. She had her phone out and was tapping away at the screen before she turned it towards him. A list of cookbooks with titles claiming to offer tasty yet healthy answers to lovers of cake.

His mouth twitched. "Thanks. Can you send me the link to that page? I might order one."

"Let me order a few. It's the least I can do."

"Are you feeling indebted to us?"

"Nope, I just want to do this."

A yawn took hold, a quick glance at his watch telling him they'd been sitting there for a few hours now. Darkness had emerged outside, even though it was only just after five. The sunshine had disappeared into dark, cloudy skies this afternoon, as if taking away the sun and happiness.

"There. I've had them sent to your house."

"Thank you. Mum will love them."

"That's a stretch, but hopefully it'll give her something to do whilst resting."

The nurse came over, letting them know they could see Barbara.

Ethan hadn't known what to expect, but his mother's

petite form hooked up to cords and looking frail was a shock.

He'd left the army to join the protection service, feeling like it had been time for him to be closer to his mum. Seeing her, he realised whilst he might have been physically closer, he hadn't been mentally closer. He'd missed the signs. He'd allowed this to happen. It was time he stepped up and was a much better son.

***

Izzie pulled Ethan's coat tighter around her shoulders. They'd been kicked out, visitation hours for Barbara officially being over for the day. The other woman had brightened considerably by the time they'd finished visiting. She'd cried at first, apologising over and over to Ethan about not having taken the medication properly. She'd realised the stakes had changed—sacrifices would have to be made in exchange for staying alive.

"Should we grab a pizza on the drive home?" Ethan asked.

She shuffled a little closer as a gust of wind whipped past them. *He must be freezing.* She was still feeling the cold snuggled into his jacket, leaving him with nothing but a short-sleeved tee. She'd argued, but he'd overridden her.

"Pizza sounds yum. C'mon. I'll race you." She took off running, realising her folly immediately, having no idea where he'd parked.

"This way." He laughed, from behind her and to the left.

She followed, her shorter stride no match for his longer one when jogging. They reached the car, puffing and out of breath. Exhilaration raced through Izzie. She couldn't be sure if it was the run or just being with Ethan. Her stomach dropped. Time to make the most of these close moments. There was a good chance Ethan wouldn't want to talk to her at all once she'd opened up to him.

Today had brought home too many familiar memories and feelings. Helping to save Barbara changed nothing about her mother's death, but in a way it had helped her realise she was stronger than she'd thought.

Hopefully Ethan would see that she was still the same person he'd met and spent the past two weeks with.

"C'mon. Stop dilly-dallying. Its freezing out here."

"You shouldn't have given me your jacket."

"I was raised a gentleman."

"That is a fact."

They grabbed a pizza on the way, the heavenly scents of pepperoni and cheese prompting a loud grumble from her tummy that was audible throughout the car.

"I may eat this entire thing by myself."

"Did you get lunch?"

"No."

"Now you tell me. I'd have ordered two."

"It's okay. I'm good at sharing."

The pizza was as good as it smelled, and they devoured it together, sitting on the couch. Ethan had opened a bottle of red, though Izzie only had a few sips before she set her glass aside. She didn't want her thoughts clouded when it was time to spill the proverbial beans.

The TV was a pleasant noise in the background, though she had no idea what was on.

All she had to do was decide where to start.

"I know I told you that my mum died, a few years ago now. She committed suicide. She'd suffered depression for most of her life and was on medication, but we found out too late that she'd stopped taking it." Her hands shook a little, and she looked around for a cushion, hoping it would give her something to hug for comfort.

Ethan switched off the TV before turning to face her. He nodded.

"I found her. The night she killed herself—I found her."

"Jesus, I can't even—"

Izzie shook her head to stop him. She scratched a finger across the light grey, textured couch fabric, unable to face the look on his face when she spoke her next words. "I found her, but I froze. I ran away, back inside. I pretended I was dreaming." Her voice shook, her words more a whisper.

The couch dipped and Ethan lifted her, as though she weighed only a feather, and brought her onto his lap. His arms cradled her gently, offering support and comfort.

"I lay on my bed, my mind twisting and turning. I'd been out drinking and dancing with friends until the early hours, and I'm ashamed to say I was not thinking straight. I don't think I slept. I just lay there in a weird trance."

It had been a long time since Izzie had allowed her mind to revisit these memories. She'd buried them in a deep, dark corner of her mind. Now she'd hacked off the lock, they were spilling out.

"You were in shock," Ethan murmured.

She searched for censure, some bit of blame or horror in his voice, but couldn't find any.

"It was my brother—Felix—who came to tell me. Even then I couldn't say anything. I just didn't believe it. I didn't want it to be true, so I pretended it wasn't. I lived in that limbo for two days until I snapped."

Izzie's throat was burning, acid bubbling and threatening to burst. She regretted the last piece of pizza she'd eaten, feeling it swirl in her stomach.

"I don't know where my brothers were, but at dinner it

was just my father and I. We were both drinking heavily. It had seemed an excellent answer to numb the pain that just wouldn't loosen its grip. I couldn't shoulder my guilt any longer and I told him. I've never seen him look at me like that. He was fuelled with hatred. And I knew I deserved it."

"Izzie, you're taking on too much blame. Depression is an ultimate killer. One man in my unit during my time in the army suffered from it. He described it as making decisions outside his rational mind. You can't hold yourself accountable."

He was trying to help. But a part of Izzie knew she'd never forgive herself for being weak that night. "He blames me. To this day, he still blames me. He can't look at me." She didn't need to explain who he was. "I received a copy of the time of death from a trusted friend the day after. By the time I'd found her, she'd been dead for four hours. It wouldn't have mattered even if I had been braver."

"But you still blame yourself."

She inhaled a shuddered breath. "Yes, and no. I know rationally that it wouldn't have mattered what I'd done. I've played the *what if* game a million times, as have both my brothers. I hate that I reacted the way I did. But even that I've learned to accept. What I can't get past is how I let my dad down. I've tried everything to get his attention, but nothing I do matters. Forever, I'll be nothing but a disappointment in his eyes. It's that, that pressure, that sense of being completely broken from his love, that I can't handle anymore. That's why I ran away."

Ethan rubbed her arms. His hands felt warm, but it didn't touch the cold that had entered her soul.

"I'm weak. I used to be strong. But now I just feel ... broken."

"Does your dad know how you feel?"

She shook her head. "I thought over time we'd find our way back. That I'd recapture some form of normal and happy. But it's like it's all gotten progressively worse."

"You're suffering anxiety attacks." It was a statement.

She glanced up then, not quite meeting his eyes but at least looking at his face to gauge his expression. "Yes. They have been getting worse. I could cover them up, but it was becoming unbearable. I'm a liability. Just before I left, there was a big event that my family needed to be at. I was late, and my dad was there with my brothers and their partners. And just witnessing how happy and open he was with them, it was like that snapped the last bit of strength I had to endure any more. I blacked out. That's not normal."

"I think you're putting yourself under an enormous amount of stress. You need to talk to your father. He needs to know what his behaviour is doing to you. You're strong. I know you are. I've seen it. Today you saved my mother's life."

She shook her head, embarrassed by Ethan's support and praise of her

"I mean it, Izzie. The nurse told me that the paramedic said if it had been much longer, my mum may not have survived. You got her the help she needed."

"I began to crumble, but I pictured your face." She looked in his eyes then, saw love reflected at her. "I couldn't let you down. I couldn't let you lose her."

His hand stroked her cheek, cautious, as though worried she'd shy away. He cupped her jaw, drawing her closer until their lips met. Sparks ignited, and she desperately wanted to give in, to just allow emotions and desires to take over. But there was more to say.

Placing her hand to his chest, she pushed back, putting space between them.

"There's more," she swallowed. *Here goes.* "My name isn't Isabella Correll. Correll was my mother's maiden name, which I used on a fake passport so no one could track me. I am ... part of the royal family. In Stenaco." She paused again, but Ethan's expression hadn't shifted. "I'm a princess."

Ethan gave a silent cheer in his mind. Izzie had opened up to him. There was only one barrier left—his telling her he already knew. She folded her lip under her front teeth, chewing on the plump skin. He tried to force the words out, but something held him back.

Izzie had just exposed her deepest and darkest issues. This was what had sent her running. Would telling her he knew who she was, and subsequently admitting how he knew, send her running again? Did he take that risk?

His gut ached, his mind swirling with the right decision, but he went with his instincts. It was too risky—she was too fragile right now. She'd placed her trust in him, telling him what she just had. Now wasn't the time to rock that boat.

"A princess," he whispered. "Guess I figured there was always something about you that made you stand out from the crowd." He offered her a lopsided grin.

"You're not angry at me? For deceiving you?"

"You had your reasons. Sometimes withholding information is the right thing to do for everyone."

She relaxed against him, like a balloon deflating. Her breath was warm beside his neck where she'd snuggled in.

"Promise me something," he whispered against her hair.

"What's that?"

"Promise you'll talk to your dad. I'm no shrink, but I

think the reason you're struggling is based around the guilt you're associating with your father."

Silence met his request, leaving him wondering if she'd ever respond.

"You're right." She sighed, her voice small. "I need him to understand that it's not fair to blame me anymore. To show him we need to find our way back to being a family, without Mum. We need to find our new normal."

"Thank you."

"Guess that means I must go home soon." She shifted, a small smile on her lips. "Will you come with me? To visit and be there for support?" Her eyes fluttered to his, then danced away.

"I want too. But I can't leave my mum. Not currently."

"Bring her. You'll both stay at the palace as my guests. I'll arrange for a private doctor. I could even see about getting a chef in to work through recipes that focus on a lighter style of living."

He shook his head, amazed at her enthusiasm and how quickly she shifted gears. "When?"

"There's a ball coming up in two weeks. How about then? That gives us more time here. I'm not ready to give this up, Ethan. Finding you … you've brought me back. You helped me unearth the me that was hiding in the shadows. What happened to my mum has broken up the family for too long. My dad needs to understand that his blaming me is breaking me apart, piece by piece. If he can't move past what happened, and understand my reaction for what it was —utter horror, denial and fear—well, then I've done everything I can."

"Does that mean I'd have to attend the ball?" He looked at her sceptically.

"Sure does, buddy. I can't wait to see you in a tux."

"A tux. So we're talking formal ball then?"

"That's implied when one says ball."

"Oh hell. Okay. Guess I better see about getting one."

"I'll hook you up."

"Hook me up, hey? That sounds dangerous." He rolled her over, trapping her underneath him. A glint crept into her eyes that spoke of pure devilishness.

"You betcha." She lifted onto her elbows and kissed him.

It was a kiss of pure passion that took them from zero to one hundred in seconds. His body leapt to catch up, igniting with fire.

"Ethan?"

"Hmm?" he muttered, unable to form a coherent response.

"Take me to bed and make love to me."

He pulled back, looking into her crystal-blue eyes that were serene and calm, like a glimmering pool on a windless day. "Are you sure?"

"Yes. A hundred times, yes."

15

*I*zzie's knees bobbed as the plane circled around in a big arc before realigning to land. The past two weeks had been a blur of heavenly spent time with Ethan and helping look after Barbara. Or more to the point, ensuring she didn't overdo things and took her medication as directed.

After her heart attack, the doctors had monitored her recovery with the correct medication, and had discharged her a few days later with instructions for bed rest and no more bickies or cake. She'd been put out, but had mellowed to contrite and then meek acceptance. She had refused to stay with Ethan and Izzie though, stating it was too much to have to live with them, but allowed them to check on her daily.

Izzie smiled, catching Barbara's quick glance from across the plane.

The view as the plane dipped towards Geravia was spectacular, and her heart skipped knowing she'd soon step foot on her home soil again. Time to stop the nervous energy and focus on the positives. Namely Ethan would be by her side and help keep her feeling strong.

The plane bumped to the ground. She was home.

Ethan shifted in the seat opposite hers, his breath hissing out.

"You okay?"

"Happy to be on land again," he responded with a wry smile.

A limousine was waiting on the tarmac when they alighted, Izzie spotting the smiling face of Felix almost instantly. She dashed down the last few steps and flew into his arms. He smelled just as she remembered, his warm embrace healing another part of her.

"Hey, sis. Nice of you to come back. Who might this stunning woman be that you've brought with you?"

Izzie looked behind her, keeping one arm around Felix's back. Barbara had bright red spots on her cheeks, her grin wide. Ethan was frowning at something over Izzie's shoulder. She turned slightly but could only see the driver and Ian. She offered Ian an apologetic smile, receiving a nod in return. She'd apologise for running off on him later. Felix had said he hadn't gotten in trouble over her disappearance, but she knew Ian would have berated himself all the same.

She turned back. "This is Barbara Raines, and her son Ethan. From Sydney. I've been staying with them."

Felix took the hand that Ethan held out, giving it a firm shake. There was an odd look that exchanged between the two before Felix shifted to give Barbara a double kiss in welcome.

"Henrik wanted to be here too, as did the girls, but schedules are hectic what with the ball only a few days away. So I'm afraid you're stuck with only me as your welcoming party."

"Only you, hey? You have changed. Previously you would have touted yourself as being the only one required."

"Yeah, yeah. Let's go. Eva's gone into overdrive and said I had to deliver you for a fitting the moment you landed. I believe you're required too, Barbara."

"Me? Heavens, what for?"

"For your ballgown," Felix replied with a cheeky grin and wink.

Izzie rolled her eyes. Apparently he hadn't changed *that* much.

The drive through the city was like a breath of fresh air. Summer was in full swing and it pleased her when the driver took them the scenic route which included driving past the markets that ran along the river's edge. The vibrant canopies created a rainbow of colour as they drove past, Izzie promising to take Ethan and Barbara for a more leisurely look soon.

The golden gates shifted inwards, perfectly timed for the limo to drive through with only the merest of pauses. Izzie glanced at Ethan, noting his expression had barely changed since they'd gotten off the plane. Was he regretting coming? Was this too much?

The palace loomed as they drove up the tree-lined expansive driveway. Manicured gardens featured on either side of the multi-storied building. The blossoms were in full bloom and Izzie was excited to explore all the gardens. Even the rose maze.

The car glided to a stop outside the double-doored entrance. Izzie was seated beside Ethan, facing Felix and Barbara. Felix was reading something on his phone. Barbara was staring out her window, eyes wide. Izzie nudged Ethan with her leg. He turned to her, a brow raised.

"All good?" she whispered. He offered her a quick nod and a half smile.

Palace staff resplendent in their maroon uniforms stepped forward to open both of the back doors.

"I could get used to this," Barbara quipped with a half laugh.

As they walked into the foyer, Izzie's name was shouted. Sophia and Eva quickly followed the noise, dashing elegantly down the double staircase. Izzie let out a squeal and ran to embrace both women.

"Oh, I missed you both," she said as she clutched them tight.

"Maybe next time you disappear you could consider taking us too?" Eva said with a laugh. "Henrik's not fit company when his little sister vanishes."

"Nor is Felix," Sophia added. "You gave them a right good scare."

Izzie pulled back. "I didn't mean to. I just ... needed some space to sort my head out."

"And did Mr Seriously-gorgeous-and-rugged-Aussie-man over there help with that?" Eva asked with a laugh.

Izzie glanced behind her. A slow smile slid across her face as she turned back to the others. "Well ... it didn't hurt, right?"

Sophia reached out and gave Izzie's hand a squeeze. "Seriously though, did it help? Can we do anything?"

"Yes, it helped. Enough of that. Let me introduce you to Ethan and his mum, Barbara." She led the two women over and made the introductions. Felix leaned in and gave Sophia a quick kiss before saying he had to go see to some work.

Izzie tried to gauge Ethan's reaction, but so far he was doing an outstanding job of hiding his feelings. She could only hope that it wasn't enough to send him flying in the opposite direction.

"Isabella."

She turned and spotted Henrik striding towards her from one of the side doors. "Henrik!"

He enveloped her in an enormous hug that left her feeling warm and yet again confirmed how much she'd missed her family.

"This is Ethan Raines and his lovely mum, Barbara."

"Pleasure to meet you, Your Highness," Ethan said, holding his hand out for a handshake.

"Enough of that," Henrik said, accepting the handshake and giving Barbara a kiss on her cheek that left a tell-tale blush in its wake. "You're our guests. Let's leave the formality for when we have to endure it. I trust your flight was pleasant, if not long? This is Stefan, my right-hand man. I'll have him escort you to your rooms. If you have questions, just ask him or any of the other staff."

"Have you taken over from the house manager then?" Izzie laughed at Henrik.

"No. She's just busy, so I offered to help. Plus, I wanted to check for myself you had, in fact, come home." His mouth held a tiny quirk of amusement.

"Your humour hasn't changed, I see." She gave Henrik's arm a squeeze, then turned to Ethan. "I'll come and see you're settled, and then I might need to disappear for a bit. I must go see my father." *Before I lose my nerve.*

Ethan gave her a nod, his eyes conveying his encouragement. Izzie ached to reach out and give him a hug but worried it might be too much in front of the current crowd. Maybe better to ease him into the situation first.

"I have an appointment with Father now if you want to come with me?" Henrik said.

Izzie opened her mouth then shut it. She was torn. She'd be abandoning Ethan and Barbara, yet her father's schedule was hectic, so turning down this opportunity could mean a much longer wait. She wanted to get this conversation over with before she lost her nerve.

"Go," Ethan said. "We'll be fine. You can do this."

Henrik gave Ethan an odd look, but Ethan's face focused solely on Izzie. She soaked in his confidence and encouragement. *Stuff it.* Closing the distance, she threw her arms around Ethan and kissed him in front of everyone, not caring who was there. He hadn't once wavered in his support of her—why on earth should she waver on her feelings for him?

"Thank you," she whispered as she pulled away. Ethan cleared his throat, looking a little uncomfortable.

"Okay, big brother, lead the way to Dad's office. I'll come find you both when I'm finished," she added over her shoulder as she followed Henrik towards the stairs. Barbara was looking smugly at Ethan, a brow raised like she'd just caught him red-handed raiding the cookie jar.

Izzie giggled, unable to help herself.

"You've found your happy, I see," Henrik said with a sideways glance.

She hooked her arm through his and pulled him close, jogging up the stairs to keep up with his longer stride. "Yes. I can't wait for you to get to know him. He's my Eva." Heat bloomed through her.

"Izzie ..." Henrik started, then paused, giving her an odd look. "We better get moving. Dad's been like a tiger with a sore foot these past few weeks."

"Is he angry with me?"

Henrik threw her a look. "No. I think he's angry at himself, and he's worried about you."

"Well, hopefully once he and I have had a proper conversation, one that is long overdue, we can put this behind us."

Henrik stopped walking and pulled her around to face him. "Is everything okay? You look happy, but honestly, Izz, you scared the daylights out of us all when you disappeared like you did. Not even Ian could find you, at first."

Izzie's stomach plummeted. "What do you mean at first?" she asked, confusion lacing her words.

"Well … let's talk about it after we've been to Dad. Maybe you can fill us in on everything?"

She swallowed, her intuition screaming that Henrik was withholding something important from her.

They walked the rest of the way in silence, their footsteps quiet on the carpeted hallways leading to her father's private offices. The ornate wooden door was closed when they reached it. Henrik gave a sharp rap against the middle. Her heart rate spiked as her father's deep voice called out to come in.

Henrik threw her a quick look, hesitating, but she wasn't having it. Instead she flung open the door and marched in, the door smacked against the wall with a bang. Time to rip off this Band-Aid.

Her father stood, his chair scraping back, his face turning from a deep frown to wide-eyed shock. "Sweetheart."

"Dad." She started, then stalled.

The door clicked closed. Her head swung towards the noise. Henrik hadn't come in.

Izzie clasped her hands together, massaging her fingers. Her nail polish had long since come off, her nails bare. How long had it been since her fingernails hadn't been buffed and manicured to perfection?

"I'm glad you came back."

She jumped at his words. Now who was avoiding looking at the other? Stealing herself, she forced her eyes to lift to her father's, expecting to be met with the side of his face or some other view. Instead, she clashed with a deep slate-blue—eyes full of pain.

"You still blame me," she said, stating a fact. She was prepared for accusation or condemnation in his gaze. She hadn't expected quirked brows of confusion.

"Blame you?" He gestured to the armchairs near the window before walking over and taking one himself. "Is that what this has all been about, Isabella? Do you feel I'm blaming you for something?"

Hurt clamoured for attention amidst her own confusion that her father could be so obtuse. "Of course you're blaming me. For Mum's death. Today is one of the first times you've looked me in the eyes without pinning me with blame."

He reeled back in his chair as though she'd slapped him. "Whatever gave you the idea that I blame you for your mother's death? Margot took her own life. She stopped her medication, didn't tell anyone she'd done so— blind-sighting us all—and then swallowed a bottle of pills."

Izzie couldn't mistake the bitter angst in his words or the utter devastation that swept across his face.

"I thought you blamed me." As she said the words, her error was clear. The truth was painted in bold letters right before her. He didn't blame her—he blamed Margot. He was angry at their mother for what she'd done, for the decision she'd made, for the hurt she'd caused—not Izzie.

He stood and turned to the window. Izzie joined him, looking out across the rose maze that spread before them. In the daylight, it was perfectly lit—each corner and swirl towards its purple-hued centre a clear path.

"I'm don't blame you. I could never blame you."

"But you can't look at me. You can't hold my gaze without getting that look of pain. Of disgust."

She turned to him then, and his shoulders slumped. She'd only ever seen her father look this beaten once before —the day of the funeral, before he'd had to walk out and show the world his face and lie about what really happened to his wife.

"You look just like her, Isabella. I'm sorry. I'm so sorry."

Shock vibrated through every vein, every blood cell, every bone of her body. Her father, the king of Stenaco, was crying. Tears slid silently down his cheeks. Clarity beckoned, like a cloak being torn from her shoulders.

"You blame her, and yourself," she said, with a sense of certainty and strength that had been lacking from her life for too long.

"I should have known she'd stopped taking the medication. I should have realised, and I didn't. Then when the unthinkable happened, I made you all lie."

She reached out and hugged her father. He turned, cocooning her in his arms, just as he'd used to. Years of worry, and hurt, and self-recriminations and self-loathing slid away from Izzie. She'd allowed this misunderstanding to go on for too long, and only now did she see how far from the truth she had been.

"That night, when I told you I'd found Mum, you looked at me with such horror and loathing. You didn't talk to me for days." The words were a little muffled, her own tears flowing freely.

He stepped back, gripping her arms and looking her dead

in the eye. "I was in a dark place then, and yes I was angry that you'd experienced that and had waited to tell me. It was like I'd failed again—my daughter was not able to talk to me about something so serious. After Margot and then that ... I just questioned everything that I was, that my most beloved couldn't confide in me. But the next day I had Ian give you the pathology report. I wanted to make sure you knew your concern was unfounded. Margot had passed hours before you found her. Miracles couldn't have brought her back to life."

Izzie hiccupped, then sobbed, then hiccupped again on a half laugh. "That report was from you?" She squeezed her eyes shut and shook her head at herself. Jeez, she was such an absolute fool. She'd spent five years living her life in a state of flux of mistaken ideas and misunderstanding. She'd pushed herself to the edge of anxiety and panic attacks, thinking her father hated her. When what she had been seeing was a reflection of his hatred of himself.

"Izzie?" Bastian's voice was full of concern, and she didn't blame him. Her body was shaking with all the emotions that were dancing about inside her.

She threw her arms around her father's neck and buried her head against his chest. She cried, eking out every drop of pain and false belief.

They stood like that, both crying for ages, and then eventually sat and talked through everything. Izzie came clean about her reasons for missing events or running from important appointments. She explained Ethan and Barbara's roles in her recovery, even telling him about her foray into bungy jumping and the exhilaration of the jet boat in Queenstown. They talked like they'd once used too, with openness and truth.

Izzie wanted to stay but she couldn't monopolise her

father's time indefinitely. Already he'd had to ask his assistant to rearrange three different other commitments.

"Isabella?" her father asked as she was leaving. "Ethan Raines is an exemplary man. I'm glad you had him to look after you whilst you went through this. I can only say I'm sorry again, a million times sorry that we got to this point."

Izzie paused over her father's high praise of a man she'd only just told him about but shrugged off the thought. "It's okay, Dad. I love you. Mum's death changed us all, but I think we've all found our way home again. Let's promise to talk properly again, from this point forward."

Her father huffed. "Since when did you get so smart and diplomatic?"

She pulled the door closed behind her and leaned against it. Izzie took a deep breath that felt like the very first inhale of fresh air, and a beginning full of promises. She'd expected to feel drained after that, but she was elated, wanting to run down the corridors and scream with happiness. For the first time in years, her life felt right. The world wasn't tilting at an odd angle, and everything was within her grasp.

More than anything, she desperately wanted to see Ethan's face. She had to tell him he had been right. That talking to her dad had given her every answer she'd ever needed. And if not for him, she'd never have found that strength.

She loved Ethan Raines. And not a thing could stop her from telling him.

16

———

*E*than paced down another corridor, his hands clasped behind him. Ornately framed paintings of past family members guarded the walls, staring at him with accusing eyes.

He'd made sure his mother was settled in before he'd left to go in search of Ian. Ian, who was Izzie's true bodyguard. The guilt was eating him alive, and yet every time he'd opened his mouth in the past two weeks to own up to his deception to Izzie, something had stopped him. A little voice in his head had told him that no, he was still protecting her.

Telling her would only hurt her.

He scrunched his eyes tight, hating that little voice.

The overnight flight had been comfortable, and the others had slept, but he hadn't been able to still his swirling mind.

He'd been to Stenaco before. Hell, he'd lived here from ages three to eight, but he didn't remember that much about it. He only remembered his dad's words that he had to go to work—it was time for him to be a hero and protect others, that they'd kick the ball around once he got back.

That memory hit him like a fist to the gut. His father hadn't ever come back.

He clutched his phone, the device ringing and breaking the unwanted thoughts in his head. "Raines."

"It's Cameron. You're a tough man to track down."

"Sorry, I'm overseas. Work thing. What's up?"

"You're good, man. Your hunch turned out to be correct after all. The wife filed a life insurance claim, one that was increased about a year ago."

"Okay. So she did it for the money?"

"Sort of. We brought her in for questioning and she cracked. Turns out your client had himself killed. He had an inoperable brain tumour. Paid his doctor to forge the medical records and hired an ex-military sniper pal. You had no chance, man. You're lucky you didn't end up dead yourself."

"He did it to protect his family."

"Yep. Anyway. Just thought you'd want to know."

Ethan hung up. He'd expected to feel a substantial weight lifted, but he didn't. He hadn't stuffed up on the job. He'd been there as a prop. His relentless pursuit of the truth had put him in a position of weakness. Hopefully, when he called his boss and explained, he could go back.

That thought didn't bring him joy like it once had.

"Ethan." The voice behind him stopped his pacing. He spun on the spot, taking in Ian and the other men that stood with him. His stomach flopped, but he made sure his expression didn't change one iota.

"Your Highnesses, Ian." He nodded. He took in the other tall man who wore the signature black suit and earpiece like Ian's. He flanked Henrik, but at a distance.

Felix rolled his eyes. "I thought we were giving formality a miss. C'mon. Standing in this corridor always gives me the heebie-jeebies. Like I'm being frowned at by years of aristocracy."

"That would be your guilty conscious talking, brother." Henrik gave Felix a droll look. The taller man shifted forward to open the closest door, but Henrik waved him off. "I've got it. Thanks, Frank."

Ethan didn't miss the slight frown that crossed the bodyguard's face. It seemed the royals felt relaxed whilst inside the palace, but he assumed they wouldn't exercise that level of laxity outside. There was enough security around that suggested whilst they were at peace, there was still always a chance of threat to the royal family.

The thought gave him a queasy feeling, not having Izzie within his sight. Not that she was his responsibility to keep safe ... Except ... dammit. That was exactly how he felt. He was kidding himself if he thought he hadn't been treating this like a serious job. Her safety meant everything to him. He'd fallen for his princess. He was sleeping with her. He'd broken every darn rule in the book, and even if it wasn't official, to him it was the truth.

Just how the heck did he explain that to her?

He walked into the room that appeared to be a library slash billiard room. The deep grey carpet was soft underfoot, the furniture an obsidian-stained wood. The colours were masculine, and he assumed it was a man cave for the brothers—royal style.

"Ethan, you look like you've swallowed a sour grape," Felix said, already relaxed in an armchair with his feet propped up on a coffee table.

Henrik's bodyguard shifted into position just outside the doorway. Ian walked across to the window and glanced out, his hands locked behind his back. Ethan had come to speak to Ian. He hadn't expected to have the royal company in tow. Did Ian plan this? Or was this a surprise to him too?

The older man turned from the window, his gaze pinning Ethan where he stood in the middle of the room. "I need to thank you for taking care of Izzie."

"Yes, allow us to add our thanks to that too, Ethan." This from Henrik, who'd walked over and sat at the gigantic table occupying the left side of the room.

Ethan felt a little on show and preceded to join Henrik at the table. "No thanks required."

"You're dismissing your role in all of this." Henrik sat forward, his hands clasped on the table, a serious expression on his face. "Izzie has been at odds ever since we lost our mother."

"She told me."

Henrik's brows rose.

Ethan chose not to expand on his comment, though he could see it was expected from the prince. Izzie had confided in him. What she told her brothers was up to her. He wasn't getting suckered into this anymore than he'd already placed himself.

"Izzie doesn't talk about Mum much," Felix added, an odd note to his voice.

Ethan could tell they were fishing. Were they sussing him out? Izzie's kiss earlier in the foyer had made the situation fairly plain. Ethan squirmed a little inside. When he'd agreed to come with Izzie, the situation had seemed easy, straight forward.

But it was far from that.

He sat in a room with two of the most powerful men in this country. It might not be his home country, but he was a guest in their palace. An old friend of his fathers, the head of their protective detail, had asked him to keep a secretive eye on the baby girl of the family. Their little sister.

He put off the intense need to swallow to bring moisture to his throat.

"You and Izzie are close." Henrik spoke again.

"If there's a question you want to ask, just ask," he said flatly.

"Is it serious?"

How the hell did he respond to that? It was a conversation he needed to have with Izzie. A conversation he'd been shoving to the back of his mind and hiding from.

For all intents and purposes, he'd only known about her true identity for two weeks. The thought of dating a princess from a royal family—from a foreign country on the other side of the world from his life—confused the hell out of him.

He wasn't ready to talk to Izzie about this, never mind her brothers. His feelings he was sure of. But the rest ... Logistically, all he could think was that it wouldn't work.

He shoved the chair back, unfathomable anger bursting through him. "Look, you asked me to keep an eye on her. I did that."

Henrik opened his mouth to interrupt, but Ethan narrowed his eyes, stilling the other man's movements.

"Hell, I jumped off a damn bridge in the name of her safety—and I loathe heights—but I did that. I monitored her every waking moment that I could. I have delivered her safely home. I don't think anything else is any of your damn business."

The room went eerily silent, the air shifted an infinitesimal amount.

Dread spread through him.

A broken sob sounded, and he spun.

There stood Izzie, frozen to the spot, her face devoid of colour and a forlorn expression of disbelief on her features. His guilt and the truth were written across his face for her to read as easily as a billboard sign. She took a step back, her movements edgy, stilted.

"No, Izzie. I can explain."

"Explain?" She gasped, pain and anguish emanating from every pore of her body. "Explain that you've been lying to me?" Her head shook, jerking from side to side. She ripped it away to take in the others in the room, every glance a pointed one of betrayal. "Let me get this straight. You all knew. You were paying him to be with me, to keep me safe? For how long?"

Ethan didn't dare take his gaze from Izzie's, though she was doing her level best not to look his way. He was encouraged to see a little colour seep back into her cheeks. She wasn't panicking. That had to be a good sign.

It was Ian who spoke. "I arranged for Ethan to be sent on forced leave for whatever duration I needed him to be at your side. If you're going to blame someone, blame me. I knew of your other passport. I knew the minute you stepped on the plane you were heading for Queenstown. I couldn't leave you unprotected, but I wanted you to have your space to work through your issues. Ethan is the son of one of my oldest friends. I used that connection. I asked his mum to help on the idea of his holiday to Queenstown."

Every word that Ian spoke fuelled the anger inside Ethan. He glared at the older man. "You set us both up."

"No. I did my job, which is to protect Princess Isabella. A responsibility I promised her mother and father I would always do, no matter what."

"What about my job? You screwed with my career!"

"No, I gave you an opportunity to take on something that freed you from the mess you'd been making at your position. You need to learn to let go occasionally, Ethan."

"I was brought up to do the job right. The charge comes first. You were my father's best friend—you more than anyone should understand that."

"Your father saw the balance in this life. You have no balance. You are all or nothing for your career. Even now, you can't admit that this was more than a job."

The words sat in the air. His own breathing echoed loudly. He turned to Izzie, who was staring at him, tears in her eyes.

"I wasn't being paid," he muttered.

Her eyes went wide and then she spun on her heel and marched out. Ethan swore under his breath and chased after her. Damn, how was she moving so fast?

She stopped, flinging herself around to face him, and pointed an accusing finger. God, she was beautiful. Her face was alive with emotion, her hair curling about her face. Even pale, she vibrated with an energy that he'd missed, even in the scant time they'd been apart.

"How long?" she spat. "How long have you known who I was? Was the bag mix-up some set-up to meet me?"

"No! I didn't know at first, okay? I noticed you on the plane before I had any idea who you were. This"—he pointed between them—"the feelings I've developed for you are one hundred per cent real. Yes, I agreed to do a favour for an old family friend, but it was outside of what I feel for you."

"How can you say that? You were protecting me. You knew exactly who I was. You saw how I was struggling and you didn't say a damn thing."

"I wasn't told what your issues with your father were. That, all of it, was you talking to me. I'm exactly the same person."

"But you were lying. I asked you if you were protecting anyone when you told me you were a bodyguard. You said no."

"That was the truth! Then."

"Why didn't you tell me when you found out?"

"You were so skittish, so odd about questions, and avoiding anything personal. I could see you were having anxiety issues. I couldn't walk away from that and I didn't want to tell you the truth in case it made you run from me. Ian said you needed help. I thought I could help you."

"Well, you did. You helped me get here, and I've resolved my issues with my father. So thanks, Ethan. A job well done. You're excused." She turned to leave.

"Wait, Izzie. Don't run away from me."

She made a sort of wounded animal noise that broke something inside him.

"Oh, I'm not running away. I'm done with running away. I'm just not hanging around for a guy who couldn't be man enough to be honest. Who put the job first. You say you have feelings for me, yet you still chose to 'protect' me by lying. We're done, Ethan. I thank you from the bottom of my heart for how you helped me get past my issues and find my strength again to talk to my father like I used to. But the lying? I can't forgive you that. Not with the ease of which you did it to my face, time and time again, and the opportunities you had to come clean? I travelled to Sydney with you —we connected. There were genuine feelings there. Even after I admitted to you about why I'd run, you could have told me then, but you chose not to."

"You'd just been through something traumatic. I didn't want to send you spinning off in another direction."

"Right. You told me I was strong, yet you lied to me rather than be honest because you thought it would weaken me? Just what's the truth there, Ethan? Either you believed in me or you didn't?"

"I didn't want to lose you," he said, and for the first time, the words felt true. Why the hell hadn't he come clean to Izzie earlier? Why had he used a flimsy excuse not to be honest?

"That's not a good enough reason, Ethan. I agonized over telling you who I am and about my past. By not returning my trust, you took advantage of my vulnerability. You're essentially saying you didn't believe I was strong enough to hear your truth."

"You're twisting my words."

"No. You're twisting the situation to get around the fact that you chose your work. You were the hero, the protector, the guardian—all of them. You chose them over just being real with me. Maybe we were both wrong to start this. Who are we kidding anyway? Even if I can get past your lying, my life is here. Yours is in Australia. Could you ever see yourself moving? I'm a princess. I can't leave again."

He didn't answer. Frustration coursed through him. This was all wrong. He'd planned to tell Izzie. He just hadn't wanted to do anything that would ruin her chance at smoothing out her situation with her father. He'd screwed it all up anyway. And what about his job?

The call from Cameron hung in his mind. He'd been right. He hadn't screwed up on the case—he hadn't stuffed up his stellar record. His job for that client was to fail in protecting him.

Could he walk away from his life there? His team? He loved his career. Didn't he?

I've taken too long.

Izzie turned and walked away. This time he let her.

I love her, but we're worlds apart.

17

Izzie thought she had run out of tears, but apparently that wasn't true. She begged off from a family dinner that night, stating jet lag and exhaustion. Her father popped his head in to check, but she pretended to be asleep. A bittersweet smile slid across her face as he closed the door behind him. He used to do that when she was a young girl. Life here had swung back around, and her relationship with her father was back to being stronger than ever. It was only a shame her heart had been a casualty in the process.

Already she felt foolish for getting so angry at Ethan over the lying. The lies had, after all, been a two-way street. What was breaking her now was the fact he wasn't willing to fight for her. For them. She'd said he'd put his job first, and whilst she'd been flinging words in anger and hurt and sheer exhaustion, now that the dust had settled, she could see which ones were true.

They'd both lied, but she'd come clean in an honest situation. She'd placed her trust and her heart in Ethan's hands. He hadn't done the same for her.

Izzie had lost her heart to a man who would always put his job first and who didn't trust in their relationship enough to risk being honest. She didn't want that for her life. From this point on, she'd only settle for truth and honesty.

The following morning, after a restless sleep, she stirred and made herself get out of bed. She'd promised to show Ethan and Barbara around at the markets. Well, she'd damn well be doing so. No way was she going to let herself wallow anymore.

Ethan had helped her get back here by believing she was strong. She was, and no lie would take that from her again. Even if seeing his face made her feel like she'd shatter into a million pieces.

Ethan rolled up another shirt before tucking it into the corner of his suitcase, all too aware of glaring eyes that threated to pierce a hole in his arm.

"You may as well speak, Mum, before your heart rate rises any further," he muttered out of frustrated at the situation along with a hefty dose of concern for his mother.

"You're making a mistake." She shot back instantly. "You need to stay, talk to Izzie."

He spun to Barbara, taking in her green eyes that were framed with a frown, her forehead lines pronounced. "I tried talking to her. I think some space is the best idea for both of us. I always knew that it would come to this."

"What, you knew you'd lie to her and break her heart?"

He shook his head. "No. I knew that we weren't destined to be together. Geographic terms alone put us on opposite sides of the world."

"So move!" She threw her hands in the air, giving him a look that told him he was daft. "Where's your sense of adventure? Geez, I thought we were related."

His mother wasn't thinking straight. She wasn't being logical. "What about you? Who'll look after you? You've just had a major heart issue. I'm not about to move away."

"Ethan Doran Raines, don't you dare put me and my health in the way of your happiness. Besides, I lived here once. I could see myself doing so again." She glanced out the window, a soft wistful smile lighting her features. "I hadn't realised until we landed yesterday how much I'd forgotten about this place. How I'd loved being here with your father."

Ethan tossed a final T-shirt into his bag, surprised at the wobble in his stomach from his mother's words. He walked over to her, crouching next to the decorative armchair she was gracing. "I wasn't sure how you'd feel about coming back here."

She turned to him, cupping his cheek with her hand and then giving it a little firm slap. "I'm fine. Quit finding excuses for your own happiness. I don't understand why you're not fighting to stay."

"Are you really happy here though?" He persisted.

"Ethan, your dad and I loved it here. Initially, when he got offered the posting, we weren't sure. How would I cope moving to another country with a three-year-old when he would be so busy with a new job? But it was fantastic. Ian couldn't do enough for us when we came out here and honestly, it's so peaceful. When we lost your dad, I couldn't face living here without him. But I've had years to come to terms with that situation. What worries me more than anything, is that you have been living under some illusion about your father. You're so committed to your job, you're not allowing anyone else in."

"That's not true."

"Isn't it? Why didn't you tell Izzie the truth?"

"Because ... well ..." Because he'd promised Ian he'd protect her and wouldn't say anything. Was that really the whole reason, though? Or was it because he was scared that he'd lose her? Which he'd done, anyway.

His phone beeped from the other side of the room. Without a second thought, he walked over and scooped up the device before reading the message from his boss. One line telling Ethan he was expecting him bright and early Monday morning, ready to get back to work.

"Well?" His mum persisted.

"I've made my decision, Mum. Let's not get into this now. I need to pack or I'll miss my flight."

"Your dad would be sad if he saw you at this moment."

Had he ever heard his mum sound so sad and disappointed? His hands clutched the phone tight before he shoved it deep into his jeans pocket. "What you and Dad had was one in a million, Mum. But he also understood that the job had to come first." His voice was tight, heat penetrating the backs of his eyes.

"No," she replied, her voice whisper-quiet but utterly clear. "That's where you're wrong. He always put his family first."

Each word was a kick in the gut. An unwanted surge of anger and frustration flooded his body. "He didn't the day he died!" he spat the words, his eyes catching his mother's whose had gone wide, her face white. "I asked him to stay and play footy. He said he *had* to go to work, that he'd come back for a game later. But he never did. He put the job first."

A lone tear leaked down his mother's face. He wanted to go to her, but was frozen by his own words, his own admission. It was like a gate had been opened inside his head, one that had been dead-bolted tight. Did he blame his father for dying? His confusion was rife. The only solid thought was that he hadn't dealt with this. Nor did he want to.

"Son, your father loved his job, and he was highly respected and good at it. But never, ever, would he have chosen it over us. What happened that day was a terrible tragedy. But he didn't choose his job, and his death, over us."

A tiny voice in Ethan's head screamed. *Then why did he go?*

"You realise that you've spent the past month looking after Izzie, helping her work through her issues, yet the whole time you've been holding yourself behind the same wall. No wonder you can't acknowledge that walking away from her is a mistake. You're still hiding."

He remained silent. Words rushed around in his head, but nothing formed into a sensible or coherent sentence.

His mother stood and walked over to him. She gave him a hug that made him feel like the eight-year-old boy he'd been the day his father died.

"I'm staying." Her words were firm.

"I can't stay, Mum. Work is expecting me first thing Monday. You should return home with me," Ethan replied, but he couldn't miss the disappointment and truth he saw reflected in his mother's gaze.

"Being here makes me feel closer to your dad, reminds me of how happy we were. I'm staying until after the ball, at least. You're hiding behind an illusion. Your father worked hard, yes, but when he was home, he was present. He let go of the job when he wasn't on duty. You don't do that, darling.

You're all or nothing and you need to find some balance." Not waiting for his reply, and muttering about his obstinance, she left the room.

Ethan finished packing and without a backwards glance, he walked out. Out of the palace, and out of Izzie's life. It was better this way.

It had to be.

A few days later, Izzie sat at her dressing table, brushing a bit of bronzer onto her face. Her complexion was still a little pasty, and given half of Stenaco's national media outlets would take official photos before the ball, she didn't want to get caught looking pale. There'd been enough speculation around her month-long disappearance from the public eye. No need to give them anything more to talk about.

She set the brush down with a little tap against the glass dish she kept her make-up brushes on. After picking up the mulled wine-coloured lipstick, she swept it across her lips.

There.

Her dress was beyond amazing. Truly, Eva had outdone herself. Izzie felt every inch the serene, calm and confident princess she'd once been. The bodice was sheer silk mesh that clung to her every curve, covered in embroidered maroon wisteria. The deep burgundy was rich in colour, her silk taffeta skirts glinting with gold thread, ballooning out for metres in every direction. It would be a showstopper, and surely that would be all the newspapers would report on.

A picture of perfection in every way.

Well, except my eyes.

She turned from the mirror that saw too much.

A soft tap at the door had her spinning on her stool as Henrik marched in. He wore a tux, his bow tie a perfect match to the colour of her own dress. Their royal colour. His face wore a frown, his hands linked behind his back. He started pacing along the end of her room.

"Come on in," she said, her tone tart, a question hidden behind the words.

"Eva and Gramps were fussing me into a lather of sweat. How do you get to escape fussing? She made your outfit too."

"Why, Henrik, you almost sound petulant."

His frown deepened as his steps stilled.

Izzie sighed. "What's wrong? How about you tell me what's on your mind?"

He turned to her, a soft smile spreading across his face as he looked at her. "You look and sound just like Mum. Those are exactly the words she would have used. That's her dressing table, isn't it?"

Izzie swallowed. "Yes. I asked Dad if I could move it in here yesterday and he helped me. It makes me feel closer to her. I think instead of hiding away from what happened, I need to embrace the memories I have of her. Celebrate what time she was part of our life instead of flinching whenever her name is mentioned."

Izzie had spent a lot of time with her father and her brothers over the past week. She'd told both Henrik and Felix everything that she'd kept bottled up. How she'd found her mother but had panicked. How she'd blamed herself and then lived with the thought that Father blamed her. How bottling all of that up had led to increased anxiety and her crazy behaviour, her eventual running away. They'd been so supportive, and now the three siblings were closer than ever before.

Unfortunately, the one man she still wanted in her life, more than anything, hadn't yet said a word. Ethan had walked out without a backwards glance. Not so much as a 'thank you, it's been fun'. Izzie had moved on from constant crying to utter rawness and feeling numb.

She had no moves left.

Only time would patch-up her heart a little, though the fractures would be permanent. Her love for Ethan hadn't dimmed in the slightest, and she feared it never would.

Felix burst into the room, energy vibrating around him and knocking her from her thoughts. He moved straight to Izzie's king-sized four-poster bed and flopped onto it like a kid throwing a tantrum.

"You'll muss your hair if you keep that up," Izzie said with a dry tone. Underneath, though, there was a bitter-sweet happiness. They'd done this as kids—piled into their mother's sitting room to hang out and share problems. Izzie had usually been mooning over some guy, or complaining about wanting new shoes. Her mother had always laughed, questioning why Izzie needed so many pairs when she only had two feet. Izzie glanced at the heels on her feet—sky-high pumps with a dainty ankle strap that glittered with crystals. Their impracticality would have made her mum smile.

"What if she says no?" Felix asked the ceiling.

Henrik raised a brow at Izzie, inquiring without words whether she knew what Felix was on about.

She shook her head. "Brother, you might need to give us context if you want an answer to that obscurity."

Felix swung his head as if only just realising Henrik was also in the room. "Why are you pacing?"

"I'm nervous. Don't change the subject. Why are you talking to the ceiling?" Henrik returned with a grimace.

"I'm planning to ask Sophia to marry me. Again. Tonight."

Izzie grinned. "Perhaps don't take it too hard if she says no. It's only been six months. She's still finding her feet with her freedom and fixing up things with her dad."

His head swung to Izzie's, and she worried he'd get a crick in his neck from the swift movement. "Are you saying I shouldn't ask her? Has she said anything to you?" His voice held panic.

"Jeez, Louise. Calm down." Izzie laughed, unable to keep her mirth at bay seeing her brother so tied up in love. "I'm just saying ask, but don't pressure Sophia. Honestly, Felix, for someone as confident with women as you were, you've become a puppy in love. Mum would have loved seeing you this happy. Both of you," she added, circling a finger in Henrik's direction.

Felix gave a soft smile, then frowned and turned back to Henrik. "Why *are* you pacing? You haven't stopped walking along the wall since I came in. Oh God. Please don't tell me Dad's stepping aside? I'm not sure I'm ready to bow down to you as a king." He mock-gasped.

Henrik shot a droll look at his brother. "Of course not. It's way worse than that. Eva's pregnant." At that bombshell, he stopped pacing and slumped into the corner chair. "Fatherhood. Impending fatherhood. What if I'm a terrible father? What if my child hates me?" His face dropped into his hands.

Elation filled Izzie, and she sprang from her chair. She raced over and jumped onto Henrik's lap, throwing her arms around him whilst she squealed with glee. "Henrik, that's fantastic news!"

"Congratulations, brother! You and Eva will make amazing parents." Felix had shifted to stand next to the chair, waiting for Izzie to move so he could pull Henrik up into a brotherly hug. Izzie couldn't help herself and jumped out, throwing her arms around both of them. She drank in their smell, felt both brothers shift to accommodate her in the hug. Her smile cracked a little, but she wouldn't let it fall. There was so much she had to be happy about at home. Even if she had lost her chance at true love, she couldn't let her disappointment shine a dark patch on theirs.

"How's Eva feeling?" she asked, her voice muffled from being crowded by both of her taller and much wider brothers.

"Good. A little tired, but no morning sickness. She has been craving hot chips, which she's given me strict instructions not to give to her. The other day when I said no to her request, she burst into tears. The contradictions will send me grey."

Henrik's smile couldn't be wider, and Izzie knew that he'd walk barefoot to the other side of the country searching for every last potato to make chips by hand for his wife if that was what she wanted.

"She's ten weeks. We're not telling anyone yet, but I had to let you both know."

Izzie's eyes filled, but she blinked them rapidly. "You will ruin my make-up if you keep talking like that."

Felix picked her up and half swung her in a circle until her dress got tangled in Henrik's legs, which sent Izzie into a fit of giggles.

"All right. Enough of this. It's time we strutted our stuff at the ball. Royal expressions on and all that." Felix quipped.

Her brothers took a hand on either side of her, escorting her out of the room.

A quick glance in her mirror showed a young lady brimming with confidence, and a carefree smile gracing her face. Now all she had to do was maintain that look for the evening and hope no one peered too closely into her eyes.

18
***

Elegant yet alluring.

Ethan's mind went off like a camera set to multi-capture shutter mode. Every second, he snapped an image of Izzie walking down the grand side steps towards the outdoor ballroom that had been erected for this twilight event. She was a beacon of light, shining in regal red, mesmerising him and not giving justice to any of his memories of her.

Had it only been a week since he'd made the biggest mistake of his life?

The flight back to Australia had been spent in tedious agony, memories flooding into his mind that he'd had locked up tight. His father taking the day off when Ethan had been sick with a gastro virus. His father turning down a job in Queensland because they had a holiday booked to the snow. His father coming home from work, exhausted after an overseas trip—but still choosing to take Ethan and Barbara out for fish and chips at the beach where they'd kicked a footy around until the last strands of sun had disappeared.

His mum was right.

He was being a fool.

He'd been helping Izzie realise that running away wasn't solving her answers when he'd been doing exactly that. He'd used one tragic memory to block out a childhood of happy memories, because it was easier than facing the loss of his dad. He'd turned his career into his life, and it wasn't until Izzie had collided with his work and his life that he saw that distinction.

Now he just had to hope he hadn't blown his only chance. Would Izzie forgive him? And more than that, would she accept him? He couldn't offer her anything that befitted her station as a royal princess, but he could offer her his love.

He stood on the far side of the raised dance floor, half hidden by a large flower arrangement. The smell from whatever was in the damn thing was strong, leaving him wishing for Izzie's far more subtle scent. But he promised himself he'd wait. She'd only just arrived, and he didn't want to pounce on her the minute she'd stepped back into the limelight. Ian had grudgingly told him about the media photoshoot beforehand and that the ball was one of the biggest events of the annual calendar. Ethan swallowed. No pressure.

"*Ah!*" He jumped at the poke to his ribs. "Mum." He scooped her into a hug.

"You're losing your touch. I walked right over to you and called your name and not once did you even flinch. So much for all that army training and elite protection service." His mum winked.

Heat passed up his neck. "I was distracted." His eyes shifted back towards his princess in red, who was now talking and laughing with her father along with her brothers and their partners. They made a striking family.

"I don't blame you. She's a worthy distraction. I'm assuming since you're here you've come to your senses?"

He turned to his mother. She was wearing a dark blue dress with a gold jacket over the top. Both fabrics looked whisper-fine and shiny. Her face glowed with happiness, and for once Ethan couldn't see the shadows that had always lurked in the corners of her smile. He ignored her question. "You're happy," he said, stating it as a fact more so than a question.

"I am. Izzie's really ensured that. She's showed me all around and even took a cooking class with me. I've found a house here." His mum's mouth twitched in a soft smile. "I went to visit the house we lived in with your father. There's another family there now with young kids. I don't know if you being here means what I hope it means, son, but I've decided to move here. Your dad was born in Geravia. We had some of the happiest years of our life in this country and I feel more connected to him here. I feel good. Healthy. I've been for a few check-ups, on Izzie's insistence, and like I told you over the phone, the medication plus the changes to my diet are doing the trick. My heart is fine. Unlike yours," she added with an arched look and a pat to his chest.

Ethan sucked in a deep breath. "You were right. I hadn't realised how much I'd become nothing but my job. I'd taken dad's last words to heart and turned them around until that was all I could remember of him. I realise now you'd been trying to say something to me for years, and how I always changed the subject away from talking about dad. I didn't let you have the enjoyment of the memories you should have had either."

His mum offered him a sad smile. "I wish I'd known

what your dad had said that day and that you've been fixated on that wording all these years."

Ethan shook his head. He'd dealt with his father's death the only way his eight-year-old self had been able to. The problem was that he'd never allowed himself to revisit the situation. Now he had. "It's in the past, Mum. I think you're right. This here is our future. It's where Dad is, and where you were happy. Now I just have to hope it's where I can be happy too."

Barbara placed a soft kiss to his cheek then squeezed him with a crazy-tight hug. "Go get your happy. It's time you found it outside your darn job."

She patted his arm, then wandered over to where Ian stood. He was dressed in his usual black and Ethan could make out a tiny ear piece hidden in his short, greying hair. Ian's eyes shifted. They darted to his with a black warning look that somehow also held encouragement, then back to where they should be—watching Izzie.

Ethan shoved his hands into his pockets. The minute he'd stepped off the plane in Sydney, he'd packed up his life. He'd put his apartment on the market, quit his job and tied up various other loose ends. He went to visit Cameron and asked after the wife. No charges had been laid against her, since her husband had ensured the entire plan led back to him. Ethan couldn't drag up another feeling about that case. He'd been so engrossed in it until he hadn't been. Until he'd realised—like the rest of his work—he'd been substituting it for his life.

He'd raced around, ensuring he'd have time to get back here to make it to the ball. And yet now he was here, he let the feelings of rushing and urgency go. He was stalling, enjoying this no man's land of wishful thinking before he worked up the guts to go to Izzie.

The band started a soft melody—a moody, haunting song. The singer's voice cut clear through the buzz of the crowd. Izzie took to the dance floor, curling into her father's open arms. When her face turned to his, her eyes were closed, her face pressed to her father's chest. A look of pure happiness graced her features. It put a light in his heart to see her at peace, even as his arms ached to be the one holding her.

He swallowed a gulp as her back shifted into view. The back of her dress was just plain, see-through fabric. The front and arms were covered in some embellishment, but not the back. His stomach dipped with memories. Of holding her in his arms. Of tasting that exquisite mouth. Of her. She was beyond beautiful and incredible, and he loved her so much.

He was ready to go all in and move here today if that won her over. He'd give her his heart, if only she'd take it.

She stepped aside to let her father dance with someone else and walked over to where Ian and Barbara stood. Ethan dragged himself from his corner, waiting for his mother to mention something, or Izzie to turn and see him. But she didn't. She spoke to Ian, gave Barbara a hug and then left. Her skirts were a trail of red behind her, a bright spark he could spot through the crowd before she disappeared into the numbers congregating on the other side of the dance floor.

He caught one glimpse of red before it vanished around the corner of the palace.

His heart knew where she was heading.

Walking with purpose, he darted through the people until he'd cleared the major crowd. He nodded to the security who lingered at the edge, dressed as party attendees. They eyed him but said nothing.

They'd have reported to Ian that he was following Izzie, which made him hope he was being given a green light. He walked through the delicate lilac gate and was assaulted with the smell of roses. The cobblestones crunched beneath his feet, his pace increasing along with his heart rate until he broke into a jog. Each twist and turn brought him closer to the middle. To her.

And there she was. Izzie, in all her glorious flaming beauty, was sitting on the wooden bench, under a canopy of blooming wisteria. Her eyes found his, widening.

"Ethan." One word, whispered.

***

Time dragged to a standstill. Was she hallucinating? Izzie gripped the bench beneath her hands, the lacquered wood-grain smooth as she pressed her thumb against it.

"Why are you here?" She forced the words past her lips.

"I'm here to apologise."

Her heart went *thunk*. She didn't want an apology.

She lifted her shoulder in a delicate shrug, her gaze floating from his. Staring at Ethan and knowing he was only here to apologise was torturous. Her body ached to go to him, but she wouldn't allow it.

"I'm sorry," he continued. "I was wrong. I was running away, and you were right. I put the job first. I knew the minute I stepped a foot out of that room, away from you, that I'd made the biggest mistake of my life. But it took me a bit to find my way back."

"What are you saying?" She didn't dare look at him, didn't dare consider anything further than the exact words he spoke to her. To hope was too painful.

"I led myself down a rabbit hole thinking that work had

to come first. That it was less painful to revolve my life around work, than live my life. Then you barrelled into my world and I fell for you the moment I saw you."

"What, bedraggled and inappropriately dressed as I returned your suitcase?"

"No. On the plane. Before I knew who you were, or anything about you. A glimpse of your back had me intrigued and then every moment I got to spend with you only dragged me in further. When Ian called and told me who you were, I tried to reign my feelings back in. I tried to tell myself that the job had to come first. That should have been easy, right? It's how I'd always lived my life. But I was kidding myself, and I hated deceiving you. You had every right to hate me after you found out the truth."

She looked up into his bottle-green eyes that were lit with hope, brighter than the lamps that studded this area. "I was deceiving you as well. You weren't the only one lying. Just because you knew I was lying, doesn't mean I was in the right. We were both hiding behind our own issues. I don't blame you for your actions."

His torso shrank and she heard his breath whoosh out, like he'd been holding his breath over her answer. He stretched out his fingers. Was he still nervous? That telling sign gave her hope.

Standing, she shifted to take one step closer. Then stopped. "Was that all?"

"No. I came back to tell you I've quit my job. I've listed my apartment. I'm moving here." He took a step closer. One corner of his mouth lifted a little.

"Moving *here*?" she repeated. "Little presumptuous. Or has Ian recruited you?" She took the next step off the centre dais.

"No. He hasn't offered me a job, and even if he does, I

won't accept it. I don't want a job protecting other people. I have nothing to offer you, Izzie. Except me." His step closer was larger this time, confidence in the move.

Izzie grinned as she took the last step that brought them right before each other. "That's lucky, because you're all I want." Reaching out, she clutched his shirt and brought him to her—her mouth finding his with eerie precision and kissing him with all she had. He matched her passion immediately, his hands sliding around her waist and massaging the skin at her back. The fine mesh rubbing against her bare skin sent goosebumps rippling across her entire body.

He broke away briefly. "I love you, Princess Isabella. The only thing I can offer you is my eternal love, if you'll have me?"

"Yes," she whispered back, before pulling his mouth to hers.

A while later, Izzie lay cocooned in Ethan's arms on the bench under the wisteria. His fingers were lazily dragging up and down her arms, hypnotic in their movements. The stars twinkled through the tiny blooms, as though winking at her from above.

"Are you really happy to move here?" she asked.

"If that's where you are," he replied. "Are you happy here?"

"Yes. Deliriously so now that you've come to your senses and returned." She giggled as he tickled her under the arm.

"Guess I better lock this in place then." He shifted, spinning her so she sat on the bench, and he knelt before her, a black velvet box held out in his hand. "Princess Isabella of Stenaco, will you marry me and make me the happiest man in the world?"

Izzie hadn't thought she could feel happier than when

Ethan had appeared, following her into her mother's rose maze, but she was wrong. A pinprick would have her exploding, she was that full of love and excitement. Gingerly, she reached out and flipped open the lid. She gasped at the solitary, enormous yellow diamond. "Ethan ... it's ..."

"Brighter than sunshine, just like you." He swallowed audibly. "That was corny wasn't it? It sounded less corny in my head." He gave her his lopsided grin that she loved so much.

After lifting the ring out, she slid it onto her left hand, then reached out and cupped Ethan's face. "Nothing would make me happier than marrying you. I love you. Corniness be damned. I love you to the moon and back, Ethan Raines, and don't you dare ever leave my side again."

"Deal," he whispered against her lips, before he kissed her once more.

"We might need a long engagement though," she muttered between peppering kisses against his lips.

"Why?"

"Felix. I'll explain later," she breathed, before distracting him in a way that didn't require anymore words.

EPILOGUE

Six Months Later

*I*zzie sniffed at the bouquet of lilies, baby's breath, roses and peonies that were bunched in her hand. Maybe she'd have peonies at her wedding. They really were beautiful flowers. Peonies and wisteria. For her mum.

The thought made her smile, as did a quick glance at the sparkling rock that graced her left hand. She twiddled her fingers, light dancing across the surface of her ring.

She sensed Ethan before his fingers danced across her back before gripping her side. "It's a beautiful wedding," he whispered at her ear.

"I've never seen Felix so darn happy. It's almost sickening." She laughed. "Sophia's just as bad though. They are so perfect for each other."

Felix swept Sophia into his arms, spinning her around on the spot before kissing her to a backdrop of flashlights. The wedding was small, mainly family and a few close friends, in the garden at the side of the palace. But both

Felix and Sophia had agreed to a photoshoot to keep the press at bay during the reception. *It surprised Izzie that her brother hadn't gone for a bigger, splashier wedding, but he'd told her this was what Sophia had wanted. And he wanted whatever she did.*

God, they are so cute.

"I hope we look that cute on our wedding day."

"Speak for yourself. I'll be looking brooding and manly," Ethan said, before turning her so she faced him. "And you'll be the most beautiful woman in the world. Which you are every day."

"I think you're getting soft in your retirement. Am I going to have to put up with this all the *time or are you ever going to go get yourself a job?*"

"*Loving you is my job, woman.*" He grinned. "*But since you mentioned it, your father pulled me aside the other day. It seems Ian's looking to retire as head of security. He's put my name forward for the position.*"

"*Is that what you want?*" Izzie asked.

"*I told him I'd have to think about it. I want to travel with you when you need to go abroad for your job. If I can't do the work whilst supporting you, then it's not for me.*"

"*You told my dad that, did you? The King of Stenaco? That you'd only accept a position he personally offered you if it fitted in with me and my plans?*"

"*Sure did.*" Ethan winked, a rakish gleam in his eyes.

"*You like to live dangerously.*"

"*Nope. I'm just protecting the woman who holds my heart and putting her first. Always.*" He leaned in, his lips soft against her, his hands sliding dangerously low considering the amount of cameras about.

Henrik cleared his throat, loud enough to show he now stood right behind Izzie. "Save that for a more private time, sis."

Ethan grinned as she broke away.

She turned to Henrik, who had Eva gripped to his side with a very prominent, perfect baby bump on show.

"Right. And just where have you two been?" She chuckled as Eva flushed a tell-tale pink, her hair now swinging loose from the braid it had been in during the wedding ceremony.

"Love is in the air," Eva said, a smile on her face directed only towards Henrik.

Izzie looked from Ethan to Henrik and Eva, and then to the happy wedded couple, Felix and Sophia. Her father stood off to the side, a contented smile on his face. He'd been smiling a lot more recently.

She dragged in another deep breath before letting it out in a slow stream as happiness replaced every part of her soul. I love you, Mum. I wish you were here. Losing you nearly broke us all, but we've found our way back. All of us—Henrik, Felix and me. I can only hope you're happy wherever you are.

She took one last sniff of the roses in her bouquet, before she pulled out the pristine snow-white one. After handing her bouquet to Ethan, she walked over to a clear patch of grass. She plucked the head off the rose and scattered the petals high into the air. A soft breeze float past her as she did so, leaving her feeling warm and happy and loved.

She turned to look at Ethan, who only had eyes for her. She'd found her happiness, forever.

THE END

PREVIEW OF LOVING LUCAS

SNEAK PEEK …

If you like your romance a little steamier, read on for a sneak peek of *Loving Lucas*: an unrequited love office romance.

Chapter 1

"What in Hell's name do you think you're doing, Miranda?"

It took a moment for her gritty eyes to adjust to the sun's

glare as she stared up at what could only be described as her worst nightmare. This was not how she'd imagined making Lucas Knight notice her. She took in his narrowed gaze, feeling her stomach flip.

"I believe it's called sleeping, but I could be wrong. Out for a morning stroll?"

Her tone was flippant, aiming to give her brain time to catch up. Not an ideal situation to be in without a large injection of caffeine. She offered up a tentative smile, hoping that might lessen the lecture she could see forming on his lips.

Lucas was only eight years older than her twenty-three, but of late he was treating her like a fourteen-year-old pesky younger sister. She was really hoping to change that situation.

"I'm heading to the office for an early meeting with your father. He asked if I could collect you from the park on the way in. I assumed he meant after you'd been out for a run, not to collect you from sleeping on a park bench." His words were clipped, disapproval written across his features.

Miranda tried to keep the smile in place, but her lips were stiff, and it felt unnatural. She'd hoped this extra measure for her university final project would prove to Lucas how determined she was to succeed at Gray Designs. She hadn't expected this level of censure.

Lucas ran a hand through his hair, causing it to stand up at all angles. "Are you out of your mind? Anything could have happened to you sleeping out here." He paused for a moment, almost like he was reigning himself in and considering a different approach. "Does your father know what you've been up to?"

Huh. Who knew anger would turn his eyes such an intense green? They were hypnotising. This man should come with a warning. Reining in her thoughts, she caught the last part of his sentence and tried to form a coherent response.

"Um... yeah, of course Dad knows. I guess that's why he asked you to collect me. I refused to let him get me, as I wanted the real homeless experience for a full twenty-four hours, which means I have—" Looking at her watch, she continued in an overly cheerful tone. "—oh... about another eight hours to go."

She didn't think his frown could get any deeper, but he proved her wrong. How did the man manage to look so appealing whilst gearing up to yell at her?

"*Real* homeless experience? Tell me you're joking." Lucas's anger skyrocketed with each word, his enunciation clearer with every syllable.

Maybe not her best choice of words.

Staring up at him, she tried a half-smile to improve the situation. "It's for my final project. I thought if I experienced a night on the street, I could better appreciate the requirements needed to design a home for—"

"So, you thought you'd sleep on a park bench? You do understand the concept of a home, right, Miranda? It generally involves four walls as a starting place."

Sarcasm laced his words, turning the fluttering butterflies in her stomach to naught. She didn't imagine the churning in her belly had much to do with hunger at this stage. *Guess he's not interested in hearing my explanation.*

She looked around, noting others still slept on the park benches that skirted this side of Sydney's Central Park. Even from a distance, she could see their clothes were dirty, their sleeping bags worn, and most slept on a smattering of tangled-up newspapers. Her conviction that this was a good idea had been solid yesterday, but having Lucas stand over her, his disapproval attacking her in waves, she had to admit he maybe had a point. Had she let her immaturity run away again? Had she thought this idea through? Her body ached with tiredness, and she'd do anything for a shower, but moreover, she just felt deflated. So much for her grand plans.

Her eyes flickered back to Lucas, who stood glaring at a spot just over her shoulder. Had she always loved him? It certainly felt that way. He'd been the first guy to pay her any attention, to really see her. Plus, he'd saved her bacon all those years ago. More recently, he just made her feel like a complete idiot.

It hurt that she couldn't even manage a friendship with him when her real feelings ran so much deeper. She wanted him to see her as a woman. He certainly didn't have any issues noticing the rest of her gender.

At the moment, his brow was raised in an "I'm waiting" expression, and she was forced to pull her thoughts back to his question. Again.

"Yes, of course, I know houses have four walls, but—oh, never mind. Let's just say there was a thought process behind the idea and leave it at that." She kept her huff to herself.

Hanging her head, she stared at the ground, unable to find the words to explain what that brilliant thought process had been. She knew it would return once he left. If only he didn't muddle her thoughts so much whenever he was around, then she could show him that she wasn't just the young daughter of his boss but a smart, sensible, mature woman.

"Perhaps then we can agree to end this *experiment,* as you call it, and get to the office? We're late."

"Sure. Actually, I might just meet you there."

"What's the problem now?"

"Shower... I kind of need one."

"It'll be a two-hour round trip to your place at this time of the morning." He shook his head slowly, like he was arguing with himself. "You can shower at mine; it's closer." He threw the words out and then strode off towards the corner entrance of the park where she could see his car was parked.

Miranda paused in the act of standing, partially because her leg had sprouted a serious case of pins and needles and she wasn't sure she could walk without falling over; however, the more pressing issue was the intense lust that had pooled inside her after hearing Lucas say three little words.

Shower. At. Mine.

How the hell was she meant to act cool and normal when he'd just invited her to get naked in his house?

Okay, so that was stretching the interpretation a little, but she couldn't help it. She wanted to do a happy dance on the spot. This would be the most time they'd ever spent alone together.

Watching the way his bespoke tailored jacket fit his broad shoulders to perfection, she hobbled along behind him. Allowing her gaze to drift lower, she came to a standstill. The fabric at his backside went taut as he lent to open the passenger door.

Hello!

Hoping she hadn't been caught ogling, she flopped into the car, murmuring a quiet thanks.

As he skirted the bonnet, she had to wonder what it was about her that brought out the worst of his attitude. He didn't snap at all the other student interns and wasn't impatient with them. Of course, they weren't related to the man who owned the company, but Lucas was always so professional with everyone else. She couldn't fathom why he treated her in such a different manner.

Having attended multiple meetings and functions together over the past few years, she'd had ample time to witness how he interacted with others. He was cordial and personable to everyone else, but with her, it always felt like he was disapproving. There certainly weren't any warm, silky smiles, like he saved for the rest of the female population, sent her way. Just once she longed to be that woman with him, to know how it felt to be held within his strong arms.

His closed-off, glacial expression said the chances of that happening weren't strong.

"So, what's the meeting about? I thought you taking over as CEO was a done deal?"

Trying to change the topic, she hoped conversation would focus her mind on something other than Lucas's capable hands caressing the leather steering wheel. Since when had she found hands sexy? Noticing them tightening in a stranglehold, she glanced at his face to see his expression had grown even darker and more distant.

Was he not happy about the situation at work? Her dad had spoken to her about his decision to take a step back at his architecture firm, Gray Designs, and hand over the reins to Lucas. She knew he'd made Lucas sign a contract stating he'd personally involve Miranda in all the relevant projects, ensuring she'd get the best training to eventually take on a leadership role.

At the time, Miranda had been more distracted by the idea of Lucas being locked into working at the company and her getting to see him every working day. Now, however, she had to wonder if he wasn't all that pleased with the idea of having to work with her.

Obviously, whatever thoughts he was having, he pushed them out of his mind as his face returned to a carefully neutral position.

"I'm not sure. Brian called last night and asked me to come in early and could I collect you from Central Park on the way in. I assumed it was concerning a new project we've been looking to bring on board. There's a piece of land south of Sydney that Live For Freedom Charity has purchased. They are building a new children's shelter and are looking for an architect who can make the most out of the space whilst being cost-effective."

"You're kidding! I didn't know Dad had something like that in the pipeline." Frowning in thought, she almost missed the weary look Lucas threw her way.

This could be perfect! It was exactly the type of project she wanted to be working on. Wondering how she could best broach the subject of working alongside him, it took her a moment to realise what Lucas was saying.

"Your father was insistent on this project."

Miranda noticed Lucas tensed as he spoke the words. "You don't agree that this is a good move for Gray Designs?"

"Do you?" His voice was carefully neutral, though it had a slight mocking tint to it.

"Of course I do! This will provide Gray Designs with a new pathway and open up the firm for new opportunities. This will show that the company is open to expanding into different areas, not just big-money projects. There is a huge market in the lower-end housing sector that we've never touched before, and I think it will add that to the company's portfolio."

"I see."

Two words. That's all the response she got? Whether it was tiredness or just his proximity, something inside Miranda snapped.

"What exactly is your problem with me, Lucas?"

That got his attention. His head swung towards her, brows raised at her outburst.

"I don't have a problem."

"That's bull. You go from smiling to having a frown greater than the Sydney Harbour Bridge whenever I enter your proximity. I have been working my butt off to prove that I'm good enough to work at the company after I finish my degree, and I'd like you to at least acknowledge that."

"Acknowledge that you're supportive of ideas that will cost the company a fortune? Pie-in-the-sky ideas that will see funds flushed down the drain on projects that would sink lesser companies. Ideas that are generated by sleeping on park benches?"

The last he muttered under his breath. But it was those words that were a real kick to her gut. She didn't know what to say for a moment and pretended to survey her nails as she worked through the array of feelings that washed through her.

"You don't have a high opinion of me, do you?"

Turning away from him, she stared out the window. Frustration welled like a fountain, and she could feel tears creep into the corners of her eyes. God, she must be tired if this was causing her to tear up.

"My opinion of you doesn't matter, Miranda, so long as you do your job."

Well, that put her in her place, didn't it? Just once, couldn't he take her seriously? She wasn't ready to give up on this.

"You know what, Lucas, I may come from a privileged

upbringing, but that doesn't mean I take it for granted and feel those who didn't are beneath me. I watched my dad build this company stone by stone, and I want to see it grow just as much as you do. I believe that projects that support charities with clever and cost-effective designs are the way into the future. A way to build the company as well as supporting the bigger projects."

Okay, that sounded a little dramatic. The words had just burst out, surprising him if the look he'd shot her was anything to go by. He shifted in his seat, clearly uncomfortable at her outburst.

She wanted to continue the conversation, get to know a little more about what he wanted for the company and let him know what she wanted to achieve there also. Make him see she would support him during his time as CEO. Have him understand they were on the same page and, more importantly, that she was going to work her ass off to be an asset to the company, not just coast along because her father was the owner. Lucas had never taken the time to have a proper conversation with her, and she was hoping this could be her chance to break down some of the invisible walls that appeared between them.

She opened her mouth to say more, but he grimaced, ending the conversation with a dark look that said there was no more to be added. He brought the car to a halt in front of his townhouse, turning off the ignition. They sat in uncomfortable silence for a few minutes. Racking her brain for a new topic of conversation, she focused her gaze up at his house.

"I love your house," she said quietly.

"Sorry?"

"Your house, I've always really liked it."

A beautiful sunlit Victorian townhouse gazed back at

her from where she sat. Just off the main street in Paddington, one of Sydney's most expensive suburbs, the quiet, leafy cul-de-sac was an ideal location. The wrought-iron gate opened out into a lovely front courtyard that was edged with hedging, creating a private and sunny breakfast nook.

She'd only been inside once—last year when Lucas had held a cocktail party there just after he'd purchased it.

But once was all it had taken for her to fall in love.

She remembered being blown away by the exterior when she'd arrived with her father, and then even more impressed by how light and open the inside was. The fully renovated inside was modern with state-of-the-art kitchen and dining areas. There was also a back courtyard with a wonderful cascading water feature along the back wall and surrounding seating amongst the gardens. It looked like a haven away from the city, and she'd wished she could have had a full tour but hadn't dared to ask.

"If I ever buy a house, I want it to be full of sunshine."

"Yes, I think I hit the jackpot with this one."

Miranda was excited to get a second look inside. She was also quietly terrified that they would be alone. What if she lost her marbles and threw herself at him? Could she blame insane tiredness for a move like that? Probably not.

Murmuring a quiet thanks to Lucas for opening her door, she tried to keep her face hidden; it felt blotchy and red—the last thing she needed him to see. Following him inside, she took a deep breath, catching his masculine scent in the air. What was it about him that dug inside her and wouldn't let go?

"Let me grab you a towel, and I should have a shirt somewhere that might fit you."

That had her pausing as she watched him head up the hallway to the linen cupboard. She was going to get to wear one of his shirts. The thought brought even more red to her cheeks, meaning she probably resembled a dishevelled beetroot.

Taking advantage of his being out of the room, she wondered if she could dig a hole in the oak floorboards and never come back out—though it would be a travesty to ruin such an exquisite floor. Kneeling, she laid her overheated cheek against the cool surface as her fingers travelled over the rustic imperfections that had been sanded and lacquered to a glossy finish.

Turning her head to cool her other cheek, she studied the intricate cornices along with the high ceilings. It was all so open and light, giving a sense of walking in the fresh air.

The interior decoration was sparse, and she knew it wasn't his own doing.

It still made her gag to think about Carmen, the interior decorator, and how she'd hung all over Lucas like a vine. Thankfully, she hadn't lasted, but Miranda knew one day one of his conquests would capture his heart, and it made her sick thinking that it wouldn't be her.

"What are you doing?"

Oh shit.

Jumping up from her position, her cheeks still flaming, Miranda opened her mouth a few times. Unfortunately, what came out, she wished back instantly.

"Yoga. I was stretching."

"Seriously?"

The dubious look on his face said he didn't buy her explanation one bit. She didn't blame him.

"Okay no, I was checking out your wood."

Oh God...

Now it was Lucas's turn to impersonate a goldfish.

"Floor! Your wooden floor!"

Wishing like hell she'd just gone with digging a hole, Miranda could feel the heat from her cheeks flood to other more private areas. Her gaze had unintentionally zeroed in on his package the minute the word "wood" had left her mouth. Had she just said that? As if being caught with her bum in the air hadn't been embarrassing enough.

"If you've finished your *appraisal,* perhaps you could get a move on?"

Work, yes, much safer topic.

Accepting the fluffy white towel and grey tee that he held out to her, she avoided eye contact as she moved towards the bathroom.

"I'll try and be quick."

Walking past him, she caught a stronger whiff of his aftershave. Something about the combination of Calvin Klein and his essential manly smell had her shuddering on the inside and escaping behind the safety of a closed door before she could embarrass herself anymore. She'd done her fill of crazy already.

Why had she agreed to come to his place to shower? Self-torture didn't suit her.

The bathroom was huge and featured a rain shower over on the far side, something Miranda herself had always wanted. Removing her clothes, she stepped under the water and let it slide over her, helping soak away some of the aches from having slept on such a hard surface. *Best to not think of hard surfaces.*

Taking advantage of the hot spray, she lathered herself with the body wash in the shower, realising too late that it must be Lucas's. Now she could spend the day torturing herself further by smelling like him.

Feeling decidedly glum after this discovery, she thought it best to cut short her shower and get going. Lucas seemed in a hurry, and she didn't want to hold him up any more than she already had.

Stepping out of the shower, she picked up the towel and blotted her face. Appreciating the fluffy texture, she did a quick survey of her reflection.

Blonde hair that fell to her midback, reasonably toned legs from the running she tried to fit in every day, and small boned—she considered herself slim rather than skinny. She didn't think her face was much to look at but didn't mind the colour of her eyes, which were a hazel green with gold highlights. She hated her dimples, which she couldn't seem to get rid of whenever she smiled. They made her feel like a cartoon character. No wonder Lucas never noticed her; she couldn't hold a candle to the stunning blondes he chose to date.

Choosing to forego the underwear she'd recently shed, she searched in the bathroom for some deodorant. Not finding any, she opened the door to call out to ask if she could borrow some and ran straight into Lucas.

Only wearing a towel, she felt immediate heat flow through her body where they touched. He must have been leaning in to knock on the door as they seemed to have stumbled into each other and were glued from chest to hips.

Holding her breath, Miranda peered up at Lucas through her lashes. The green in his eyes was so deep it was almost black, taking on a predatory gleam as his gaze locked with hers. Her breathing was shallow and uneven, mingling with the minty freshness that was exuding from his mouth.

Trapped by the seductive spell woven by his proximity, she couldn't move. Didn't want to move. Such was the power of the feelings that enveloped her. A tingling sensation washed across her breasts where the rough texture of the towel pressed against her, captured between the two of them.

He had steadied her after their collision, and she could feel his arms at her sides, his fingers gripping her hips tightly. Mesmerised by the electric sparks flowing between them, she watched his gaze dip lower, taking in her bust, which had taken on a heaving quality from being pushed up between them.

His eyes flicked back to hers, and she felt his intense desire, clearly evident from the large bulge pushing against her stomach.

"Damn." Lucas closed his eyes and took a step away.

It took Miranda a moment to realise the insistent ringing in her head was a phone coming from the lounge room. She felt bereft as he walked away.

Maybe he's not that indifferent to me.

CLICK HERE TO READ ALL OF LOVING LUCAS

STAY CONNECTED

Never miss a new release or give away! Sign up to Jayne's newsletter here to stay in the loop.

And if you loved this book, please take a moment to leave a review once you're done.

Thank you!